PEN PALS: BOOK FIVE

SAM THE SHAM

by *Sharon Dennis Wyeth*

A YEARLING BOOK

Published by
Dell Publishing
a division of
Bantam Doubleday Dell Publishing Group, Inc.
666 Fifth Avenue
New York, New York 10103

The trademark Yearling ® is registered in the U.S. Patent and Trademark
Office.

ISBN: 0-440-40250-6
Published by arrangement with Parachute Press, Inc.
Printed in the United States of America
December 1989
10 9 8 7 6 5 4 3 2 1
OPM

CHAPTER ONE

"Hurry up!" Lisa McGreevy shouted, looking out the window of Suite 3-D of Fox Hall at the Alma Stephens School for Girls. "Shanon and Miss Grayson are out front with the van."

In the next room, Palmer Durand fluffed her wavy blond hair irritably. "I'm coming. The way you're carrying on, you'd think this was a big deal or something."

"It is," Lisa reminded her, "for the kids in the Brighton Project. They're only in third grade. They probably look forward to meeting with their tutors."

"Well, I wish *I* could say the same." Palmer stepped out of the bedroom she shared with Amy Ho, the fourth resident of their suite, and into the sitting room. "This tutoring business is getting to be a bore," she announced, giving her head a final shake.

Lisa moved away from the window and sat down on the pink loveseat. Her rich brown eyes were solemn as they followed Palmer's slow-motion preparations. "If you weren't serious about helping those kids from the Brighton elementary school, you shouldn't have signed up as a tutor."

"You know we're required to take part in a community service project each semester," pouted Palmer. "What did you expect me to do? Help clean up the trash from that vacant lot on the other side of town?"

Lisa eyed her suitemate's spotless pink cotton pants and matching cropped sweater. "No, Palmer," she agreed with a wry smile. "I don't suppose you'd ever volunteer for anything that might get your hands—or your clothes—dirty."

"I considered visiting the nursing home, like you and Amy, but you know I can't stand being around old people." Palmer shivered dramatically. "They give me the creeps."

Lisa threw up her hands. Palmer was hopeless. Sometimes it seemed she never thought of anyone but herself. Still, her closest friends knew she wasn't quite as selfish as she sounded. She'd had her share of problems, and she was sometimes most sensitive when you least expected it.

From the street outside the dorm, a horn blared.

"Miss Grayson is going to be angry if you don't stop messing with your hair and get downstairs," Lisa said.

"I'm on my way," Palmer replied, sauntering toward the door.

Just before her hand touched the knob, the door flew open and Amy Ho burst into the room. As usual, she was dressed all in black. Black T-shirt, black jeans skirt, and black mini-boots. Her jet-black hair was moussed into a wild punk hairdo.

"Mail call!" she cried. Hurrying across the room, she dropped an armload of envelopes onto the little table in front of the loveseat.

"I'll bet they're all for me!" Palmer cried, gleefully reversing course.

Amy rolled her eyes. "*Our* pen pals might have written to the rest of us too."

"Well," Palmer admitted, "I suppose there might be one for each of you. But there must be twenty or thirty letters here." She sat on the loveseat and seized one of the envelopes, a pale blue one.

All the girls in Suite 3-D looked forward to the mail each day. Early in the semester, they thought they'd found the perfect solution to the total lack of male companionship at the all-girl Alma Stephens . . . the nearby all-boy Ardsley Academy! Unfortunately, even though Ardsley and Alma were only miles apart, there were few opportunities for socializing. Telephones at both schools were almost as hard to get hold of as rides between campuses. And to make matters worse, the freshman girls—third-formers as they were called at Alma—weren't allowed off campus without a chaperone.

But that hadn't stopped Amy, Palmer, Shanon, and Lisa. Code-naming themselves Foxes of the Third Dimension, they had simply placed an ad in the Ardsley newspaper, seeking boy pen pals. Out of the many responses they received, they had chosen four suitemates from Ardsley who called themselves The Unknown.

All the Foxes had been thrilled with the arrangement—except Palmer. She'd quickly rejected her own pen pal, John Adams, in favor of Amy's—the rich and handsome Simmie Randolph III. But almost as quickly, Simmie had dumped Palmer for a girl from another school. And though Simmie later tried to get Palmer back, she'd wanted no part of him.

After Palmer's disappointing experiences with her first two pen pals, her suitemates had decided to place another ad in the Ardsley newspaper seeking a replacement. Judging from the response, there were plenty of boys interested in writing to Palmer. Of all the girls at Fox Hall, she was the most strikingly beautiful.

Now, as Palmer started to open the pale blue envelope, Lisa ran across the room and snatched it out of her hand. "Palmer! Aren't you forgetting something?"

"Huh? What?"

Amy laughed. "The Brighton Project! You can read your fan mail when you get back!"

"I have to wait two whole hours?" Palmer wailed.

"Sorry," Lisa said firmly. "Duty calls."

Tossing the letter back onto the pile, Palmer groaned with frustration.

"I wonder . . ." Amy muttered.

Palmer spun on her roommate. Amy was holding a mysterious black envelope up to the sunlight.

"Don't even think it, Amy!" Palmer warned. "This is *my* mail. *I* will open it when I get back, and I don't want anyone else touching it until then." Heading toward the door once more, she called back over her shoulder, "Don't you so much as *breathe* on those letters!"

Amy groaned as her blond suitemate disappeared out the door. "She sure is touchy."

Despite Palmer's parting words, Lisa immediately began sorting through the envelopes. She was eager to see if her own pen pal, Rob Williams, had written. Luckily, she and Rob had hit it off from the start—first in their letters and then at an Alma school dance. As far as Lisa was concerned, Rob was even better in person than he was on paper. He had dark curly hair, almost the same color as her own, and brilliant blue eyes. She thought about him every day and could hardly wait to see him again.

"Any of those for me?" Amy asked hopefully, thinking of her own pen pal, John Adams.

"No." Lisa sighed. "Every single one's for Palmer. She'll be thrilled."

Meanwhile, Palmer was looking anything *but* thrilled as she climbed into the school van and found an empty seat behind her other suitemate, Shanon Davis.

Shanon turned around and peered at Palmer, her hazel eyes puzzled. "What took you so long?"

"The mail came."

Kate Majors, a fifth-former and dorm monitor for Fox Hall, shook her head knowingly. "And when the mail arrives, the Foxes drop everything."

"That's not true," Shanon protested. "I take my tutoring very seriously."

"We know you do," Miss Grayson said, as she steered the van away from the curb and into the light traffic passing by the school. "You seem to be making some real headway with your student. Her teacher told me that she's seeing marked improvement in Petra's writing skills."

"Really?" Shanon exclaimed, pleased.

"Absolutely," said Miss Grayson. "I think all the children are benefitting from the program."

"Not mine," Palmer complained. "Gabby must be slow or something. She doesn't seem to understand a thing I say."

"You're not very patient with her," Kate pointed out. "I've heard you working with her."

"I *am* patient!" Palmer snapped impatiently. "It's just that she won't pay attention. She even admitted that she hates arithmetic."

"Knowing how *you* feel about math, I'd think you would sympathize with her," Shanon said quietly.

"And that's another thing," Palmer complained. "I don't think I should be tutoring anyone in math. It's my worst subject."

Miss Grayson turned the van down a narrow street and parked in front of a large brick building—the town library. "Haven't you mastered third-grade math yet, Palmer?" she asked with a teasing smile.

"Of course I can do third-grade math," Palmer sputtered. "That's not the point. Gabby just isn't trying. I mean, her parents sure picked the right name for her—the kid never shuts up!"

"Well, some of us take a bit longer to catch on. Keep

trying. I'm sure you'll get through to her," Miss Grayson said gently.

Palmer tried her best that afternoon. "Come on, Gabby, concentrate," she said, tapping her pencil tip on the sheet of addition problems in front of the little girl.

Gabby wriggled in her chair. "I need a drink of water."

"You've had three drinks in the past fifteen minutes," Palmer exclaimed.

"I'm thirsty," the freckle-faced little redhead whined.

"Oh, all right, go get your drink!" Palmer leaned back in her chair in exasperation.

"Now, are you ready to work?" she asked when Gabby returned to her seat several minutes later.

The third-grader studied her pencil with a flicker of a mischievous smile. "I need to sharpen my pencil now," she said, and was up and out of her seat again before Palmer could stop her.

"Oh, good grief," the reluctant tutor groaned.

Gabby's restlessness soon began to rub off on Palmer, who kept watching the clock while her thoughts drifted back to the tempting pile of letters waiting for her at the suite. All those boys wanted to be her pen pal. How could she keep them waiting like this?

At last, the tutoring session was over. The elementary students were gathered together by their teacher, and then Shanon and Palmer followed Miss Grayson and Kate out to the van.

"Listen to this," Shanon exclaimed as they started back to the school. " 'My dream. I want to be a ballet dancer and travel all over the whole world. I would wear a sparkly white princess costume and float across the stage and make people happy by dancing a beautiful dance for them.' Isn't that sweet?"

Palmer glared at the piece of notebook paper in Shanon's hand. "Let me see that." Her blue eyes swept over the words. "This is terrible. Every other word is misspelled."

Shanon timidly took back the paper. "Petra wrote it all by herself. She may not spell very well, but she wrote in complete sentences, with capital letters at the beginning and periods at the end."

"Big deal," Palmer said.

"It is for Petra," Shanon insisted. "You should have seen how she started out a few months ago. She could barely spell 'cat'!" Shanon swept her light brown braid back over her shoulder. A local girl, like Petra, she couldn't help identifying with the youngster. Shanon knew very well she would never have wound up at the expensive Alma Stephens boarding school without the academic scholarship she'd worked so hard to win. Palmer, it often seemed, had no need—and no desire—to work hard at anything.

As Miss Grayson drove down the main street of town, still a mile from Alma Stephens, Shanon leaned back in her seat and closed her eyes. There was no point in talking to Palmer when she was in one of her moods.

"Can't you drive any faster?" Palmer urged, leaning over Miss Grayson's seat.

"Not without breaking the speed limit." The popular young French teacher, who lived as an advisor in Fox Hall, cast a curious glance at Palmer. "Anxious to get back to your own studies?"

8

"Mmm," Palmer said, staring dreamily out the window, "something like that."

Ten minutes later, all four girls were gathered in a circle on the sitting-room floor of Suite 3-D. Palmer arranged the letters in front of her according to color so that they looked like a rainbow.

"Well," Lisa prodded, "start reading."

"I will, I will," Palmer said. "Don't rush me. This is a very important moment in my life. Who knows what sort of boy I may meet."

Despite Palmer's haughty attitude, Lisa was glad to see the sparkle back in her friend's eyes. Though all the Foxes had applauded Palmer when she stopped speaking—and writing—to Simmie, they'd soon learned that a Palmer without a boy in her life was not the most pleasant person to live with. Somewhat self-absorbed and huffy in the best of times, she could be absolutely impossible when the going got tough.

But now, fortunately, things seemed to be looking up.

"Just *pick* one!" Amy pleaded. "I can't stand the suspense."

"All right." Palmer, surprisingly, reached for the black envelope. The other girls held their breath. But she didn't open it. Instead she tossed it into the wastebasket she'd dragged out of her bedroom.

"What did you do that for?" Lisa demanded. "You didn't even read it."

"I can tell he wouldn't be my type," Palmer said. "He's probably an undertaker's son, or something just as gross."

9

"I thought it looked interesting," Amy murmured, her eyes drifting wistfully toward the wastebasket.

"You would," Palmer groaned, giving Amy's all-black outfit a disdainful look before picking up the blue envelope she'd nearly opened a few hours earlier. Carefully, she ran one pink-polished thumbnail under the flap, then peered inside.

"Come on, come on," cried Shanon, bouncing up and down on her knees.

"Quiet, children." Palmer took a deep breath and started reading.

Dear Palmer,

I like your name. I want to be your pen pal. We could make a swinging twosome. Here's my picture, since you asked for it in your ad.

Signed,
Arnold

Lisa hooted. "Arnold! Get it? Arnold Palmer—the famous golfer!"

"And look at his photo!" Amy said. "He's swinging one of those goofy, oversized plastic clubs."

"He looks like a total nerd to me," Palmer ruled, tossing the letter aside.

"Oh," Shanon said. "I think he's cute."

"There are plenty of other fish in the sea," Palmer proclaimed, snatching up a plain white envelope with large printed letters in bold, black ink. "This one looks more forceful. I like the strong type."

She read it silently, then threw it into the trash too.

Lisa grabbed for the letter. "Hey, wait! We didn't get to hear it."

"Forget it! I'm not interested. Imagine—he wanted me to go bicycle riding with him around the lake."

"What's wrong with that?" Amy demanded.

"Can you see me and some boy pedaling around the lake, all hot and sweaty? That's just not me."

"I agree," Lisa said with a straight face. "Being seen like that could definitely ruin your image."

Palmer didn't seem to realize she was being teased. "At least you understand me, Lisa. You choose the next one. Which do I open?"

Palmer quickly ripped open ten more letters, none of which met with her approval. But then, at last, she found one worth sharing. "Listen to this," she said.

Dear Palmer,

My name is Sam O'Leary. Here's my picture. Hope you think it's okay because I'd really like to be your special friend. My interests include sports (I play lacrosse, and swim, and ski). I like dancing a lot, too, but I don't get to do it much because I'm too busy making music. I've played the guitar and drums since I was six. Now I have my own rock band. A lot of girls think it's cool to hang around with musicians for the prestige. I want to find a girl who likes me for myself.

Please write,
Sam

11

"Oooh, he sounds really nice," Shanon said.

Palmer blinked, studying the letter. "He does, doesn't he?" she mused.

"Are you going to write to him?" Lisa asked.

"I don't know," Palmer said uncertainly. "I mean, he sounds great. But so did Simmie. How do I know he didn't just make up all this stuff about having a band?"

"Look at his photo," Amy said, picking it up off the floor where it had fallen when Palmer unfolded the letter. "Does that look like the face of a liar?"

"No," Palmer agreed slowly, gazing into a pair of wide-set gray eyes that looked out from under a thatch of reddish curls. "I guess not. He is kind of good-looking."

"What are you talking about?" Lisa cried, looking over Palmer's shoulder at the snapshot. "He's an absolute hunk!"

"So was Simmie. And you all keep telling me that looks aren't everything!" Palmer said smugly. "Besides, I'm not sure I care for his name."

"His name?" Amy asked.

"Sam O'Leary. He sounds like a leprechaun. Maybe he's the type that likes to play mean tricks on girls."

"You're just searching for excuses not to take a chance," Shanon guessed. "You've got to try, if you want to find someone new. What happens at the next dance? We'll all have dates, and you won't."

Palmer straightened up, her eyes flashing. "That'll be the day!"

"Then you'll write to him?" Lisa asked.

Palmer took a deep breath and studied Sam's picture for

12

a minute. At last she smiled brightly. "Hey, what have I got to lose? I can't do any worse than Simmie Randolph the Third, can I?" She jumped to her feet and spun around, her blond hair swinging in a golden blur. Waltzing out of the sitting room with Sam's letter and photo, she left the discarded notes for the other girls to pick up.

"That's the old Palmer we know and love," Amy said with a laugh.

CHAPTER TWO

Dear Sam,

   I want to sort of clear up a few things before I accept you as my pen pal. Did you mean in your letter that you actually are the leader of a rock band that plays at real dances? A lot of kids just fool around with instruments, like my roommate.

   If you are a pro, I think that's really neat. Not that I'm one of those silly groupies you mentioned. I'd never be like that.

Sincerely,
Palmer

P.S. I understand rock musicians make a lot of money. Is that true?

Dear Palmer,

   Yes, I'm definitely the leader of my band. We're called The Fantasy, and I guess you could say we're professional musicians because we get paid. As far as whether it's a lot

14

of money—I never really thought much about it. Compared to what other kids earn, I suppose we do make a lot.

                                                    Yours,
                                                    Sam
P.S. I'm sending you a tape so you can hear what I sound like as well as see what I look like.

"I can't believe how lucky you are, Palmer," Lisa said with a sigh. "A rich hunk rock singer for a pen pal."

"I think the most important thing about Sam is that he sounds nice," Shanon pointed out.

Amy nodded. "And he's clever, too. He thought of sending you a tape. I wonder what he sounds like."

"Fantastic, I'll bet," Lisa sighed, rolling her eyes up at the blue spring sky overhead. The four girls had deserted their suite for the grassy quad between dorms on the Alma campus. The temperature was supposed to hit seventy that afternoon, and a scent of summer was in the air. One group of girls seated nearby was passing around suntan lotion for their arms and legs. "If Sam's voice is anything like his face, he'll sing like an angel."

"Hey, wait a minute!" Palmer cried, standing up with Sam's letter clutched possessively in her hand. "Whose pen pal is he anyway?"

"He's all yours, Palmer," Lisa said. "I'm perfectly happy with the one I've got."

"Me, too," Amy agreed quickly.

"Me, too," Shanon echoed. "I wouldn't trade Mars for anyone."

15

"Well, I hope you remember that when you see Sam in person. I don't want you hanging all over him like sappy groupies, just because he's a star."

"He didn't say anything about being a star in his letters," Lisa objected.

"I'm sure he's too cool to brag about himself," Palmer said haughtily, starting to walk away from the others.

"The bigger they are, the nicer they are," Amy muttered under her breath.

Lisa and Shanon giggled. Palmer kept on walking.

"Hey," Lisa yelled, "where are you going?"

"Where do you think?" Palmer yelled back. She waved the tape in the air.

In a flash the other three girls were on their feet, running after her.

"You aren't going to play that tape without us," Amy called as Palmer dashed into Fox Hall.

Shouting at Palmer to stop, they pounded up the steps and down the corridor after her. Palmer beat them to the suite and, laughing, locked the door behind her.

"I don't have my key!" Amy wailed, hopping up and down in frustration outside the door.

"I do." Lisa reached into her purse, but before she could open the door Kate Majors stepped out of her room.

"What's all the noise about?" the older girl demanded. "I'm trying to study for a French test."

"Sorry, Kate," Shanon said. Though the other girls considered Kate a little too bossy at best—and a total dweeb at worst—Shanon had come to like and admire her. Working together on the Brighton Project as well as on the

16

school newspaper, *The Ledger,* the two girls had found they had lots in common.

Shanon gave Kate an apologetic smile as Lisa began fumbling with the key in the lock.

"Palmer has a new pen pal," Amy explained.

"He's a rock musician, and he sent a tape of his band."

"Really?" Kate asked, stepping hesitantly into the hall. Her eyes glowed with interest. "You know, I play a little guitar myself. Nothing great of course, but . . ."

"Why don't you come in and listen to the tape with us," Shanon suggested. On second thought, she glanced at the other girls.

"Sure," Lisa said grudgingly, at last getting the door open. "Come on." Kate and Reggie, Lisa's brother who was at Ardsley, had started writing letters earlier in the year. And Lisa, who'd never cared much for Kate, seemed to like her even less now.

As the girls burst into the sitting room that separated the two bedrooms, they could hear loud music coming from Amy and Palmer's room.

"Follow that drum beat!" Amy cried, leading the charge.

Since the interior doors didn't lock, Palmer had attempted to barricade her bedroom door by pushing Amy's bed against it. However, with four girls pushing from the other side, it didn't hold for long.

Palmer smiled at them mischievously when they slid through the narrow opening, one by one. "What took you so long?"

"My, *she's* in a good mood," Kate commented wryly.

"Just pipe down and listen to this," Palmer said.

17

The four Foxes and their neighbor crowded onto the twin beds and concentrated on the music blaring out of Palmer's tape deck.

"Someone's playing a mean bass guitar in there," Amy commented appreciatively.

"I love the drums," Shanon said, blushing. "They're like a pounding heartbeat."

"The keyboard player isn't bad either. Which instrument is Sam playing?" Lisa asked.

"Shhh!" Palmer said. "I can't hear if you're all going to talk."

They listened in silence for the rest of the instrumental number. The second song was much softer and slower, and it featured romantic lyrics sung in a husky male baritone.

"Is that Sam?" Shanon asked, mesmerized.

Palmer pretended to swoon, falling back on the bed with her pillow over her face. "Huvem," she mumbled from beneath it.

"What?" Amy asked, lifting the pillow from her roommate's face.

"I said HEAVEN!" Palmer shrieked, beaming at them. "I'm in love. I can't believe this is happening to me. He's so-o-o-o perfect!"

"He does have a great voice," Lisa agreed.

"I think he's extremely talented," Kate added.

After two more numbers, the tape ran on silently.

"I think that's it," Amy said. She ejected the cassette from the machine and handed it over to Palmer.

Palmer sat on her bed, gazing down at the tape in her hands, as if in shock. "Sam's band really is good, isn't it?"

18

"I think they're great," Amy said. "I wish we could get them to come play for an Alma dance."

Palmer laughed.

"What's so funny?" Lisa asked.

Lifting her chin, Palmer stared down her nose at Lisa. "What makes you think a slick band like The Fantasy would agree to play at some old girls' school in the middle of New Hampshire. I'll bet they do gigs at nightclubs and resorts, maybe even in New York City."

"They're good, Palmer," Amy admitted, "but I'm not sure they're *that* good."

"Oh, how would you know?" Palmer retorted. "You can't even carry a tune."

"Hey," Lisa said, coming to Amy's defense, "that's not very nice, and it isn't even true. Amy's got a great voice, and she plays the guitar really well."

Amy shot Palmer a hurt look. "My voice *is* sort of . . . unusual, though. I'm sure some people don't think I sing very well."

"Unusual is good, in your case," Shanon assured her. "Your voice suits you."

"If she were really any good," Palmer commented, gazing at Sam's photograph while she lay on her bed, "she'd have a band, or at least be *in* a band."

"Knock it off, Palmer," Kate warned. "Just because things are going your way now, doesn't give you a license to be mean to people."

"Jealous?" Palmer said slyly. "I think you're all just jealous because your pen pals aren't as cool as Sam."

"Oh, good grief," Lisa groaned.

19

After supper that night, Shanon left for the *Ledger* office to meet with Kate. Lisa and Amy agreed to test each other on their Latin vocabulary for a quiz the next day.

"Where do you want to work?" Lisa asked.

"The sitting room, I guess," Amy said, sounding unusually subdued.

"We can use the study lounge downstairs," Lisa suggested.

"No, that gets pretty crowded," Amy sighed. "I'm really nervous about this test. I'd like to just stretch out on my bed, close my eyes, and sort of imagine the word list. That usually works pretty well for me. But Palmer seems to have taken over our bedroom."

"You could lie down on the loveseat."

"Somehow I don't think it would work, with the . . . well, you know. . . ." She waved her hand toward her bedroom door.

From the other side a drumbeat throbbed.

"That must be the hundredth time she's played Sam's tape," Lisa said, shaking her head.

"At least," Amy agreed. "I'm getting a little tired of The Fantasy."

"She should be more considerate of the rest of us."

"Palmer?!" Amy snorted.

"You're right. In her case, that would be a lot to ask."

"It would be a miracle," said Amy.

"Well, if we go into *my* bedroom, that'll leave the sitting room between us and the music lover."

Amy nodded. "Let's give it a try."

But even in Lisa's room, the sound of wild rock music was only somewhat muffled. "Okay?" she asked.

Amy gave a sigh. "Guess it'll have to do." She plopped down on Shanon's bed, opened her Latin text to the right page, and handed it to Lisa. "Mix up the words so I don't just remember by the order they're in."

"Gotcha."

They'd barely begun when Palmer burst through the door, letting in a blast of guitars. "So there you are," she said. "I've been looking all over for you, Amy."

"For me?" Amy raised a questioning eyebrow. "I thought you'd forgotten who I was."

"Don't be silly," Palmer said. "How could I forget my own roommate?" She gave Amy a bright smile before going on. "Listen, I have a really important math test tomorrow. You've got to help me with it."

"Now, wait a minute," Lisa broke in. "*She* has to help *you?* After what you said to her before?"

"Me? What did I say?" Palmer demanded, looking honestly confused.

"You insulted her music, her voice, her guitar playing."

"Oh, that! I didn't mean anything by it," Palmer insisted. "It's just that once you hear a professional work, you notice the difference. An amateur like Amy has a long way to go."

Amy and Lisa both glared at her.

"All right, all right," Palmer said quickly. "So maybe you are pretty good. It's just that . . ." Her voice faded off and a dreamy look came into her eyes. "Did you know that the last song on that tape was dedicated to me?"

21

That was too much for the other two girls.

"Honest?" Amy gasped.

"How romantic," Lisa said, sighing deeply.

"Isn't it?" Palmer shook her head, laughing, her eyes glowing. "Sam *is* a fantasy. But I've been so wrapped up listening to his tape, I completely forgot about my homework. All the rest can wait, but not the math test. I have to pull at least a B or my final grade is going to be a D!"

"I don't know," Amy said doubtfully. "It's already after nine o'clock. Lights out in less than an hour."

Palmer dropped her head, her blond hair falling over her eyes. "Please, Amy," she wheedled. "You're my only hope."

"Oh, all right," Amy said good-naturedly as she jumped up from the bed. "If you promise to turn off the tape and really concentrate, we can get a lot done before lights out. Then your brain will work subconsciously while you sleep. You'll be surprised what you remember in the morning."

Palmer beamed at her roommate. Then, in a move that surprised all three girls, she reached out and gave Amy a big hug. "You're the greatest."

Amy's face turned red. "You're not so bad yourself."

At lunch the next day, the four Foxes gathered at their usual table in the middle of the cafeteria.

"How was the math test, Palmer?" Amy asked as she set her tray down.

"No sweat." She took a sip of juice before adding, "I'm sure I did great. I don't know what I was so nervous about."

22

Lisa shot Amy a look, then glanced back at Palmer. "Aren't you even going to thank Amy?"

"What for?" Palmer said blithely. But when all three of her suitemates groaned, she added, "Oh, you mean for the tutoring? Sure. Thanks, Amy—you're a real friend. I don't know what I would have done without you."

"Forget it," Amy said. "Besides, I have something more important to talk to you all about."

Lisa looked up from her tuna sub, intrigued. "What is it?"

"Well," Amy began, popping a potato chip into her mouth, "I've been thinking. It's been a while since we've seen our pen pals, and we've *never* seen Palmer's pal, Sam."

"That's true," Lisa replied. "But getting together with the Ardsley boys won't be easy. The next Alma dance isn't for ages."

"I know. That's why I thought everyone would be interested in this!" Amy took a bright orange sheet of paper out of her book bag and laid it on the cafeteria table. "There's going to be a one-day geological seminar with some visiting college professor at Ardsley Academy. Students from all the nearby schools are invited to sign up for it."

"Geology?" Palmer wrinkled her nose. "Aren't geologists those weird guys who go crawling around on the ground, smacking rocks with little hammers?"

"I think they do a lot more than that," Lisa commented dryly. "If you come to the seminar, you'll find out."

"And you'll get a chance to see Sam," Amy added.

"I will?"

"And the rest of us will be able to see our pen pals, too!" Shanon said, catching on.

"How do you figure that?" Palmer asked skeptically.

"Easy," Amy said. "All we have to do is write to our pen pals, tell them we'll be signing up for the seminar, and ask them to do the same. That way we'll get to spend almost a *whole afternoon* together!"

Palmer tilted her head to one side, considering. Finally she smiled. "That's not a bad idea. I think I'll do it." Then her face grew solemn again. "I just hope Sam will go for it. I mean, a geology seminar. How exciting can that be to a rock star?"

"What could be *more* exciting to a 'rock' star?" Amy teased.

"If he wants to meet you, he'll come," Lisa pointed out.

Palmer grinned. "You're right. He wouldn't pass up a chance like that, would he?"

CHAPTER THREE

Dear Shanon,

Thanks for letting me know about the geology seminar. I signed up for it today. Did I tell you that I once invented a rock tumbler? You know, those things you put plain pebbles in, and they turn round and round and days later come out all smooth and pretty. Anyway, it was hamster-powered, so it only worked when my hamster Taco was on his exercise wheel. Unfortunately, he usually got tired before the rocks were finished. What I really needed was a whole fleet of hamsters, but my mother vetoed the idea. So much for my experience in geology. Anyway, this should be fun. See you there.

> Spinning in circles over you,
> Mars

Dear Lisa,

Geology? If anyone else had asked me to spend my free afternoon in a lecture hall listening to some old fossil (ha!)

talk about rocks, I'd have said they were crazy. But since you'll be there—so will I, for sure!

Signed in granite,
Rob

P.S. Actually this might be interesting. I collected a bunch of rocks while I was in Alaska last summer. I never found out what some of them were. Maybe I'll bring them along.

Dear Amy,
   You can bet your guitar I'll be there. It won't be easy, though—I have baseball practice scheduled for two o'clock. But don't worry, I'll find some way to get out of it. Can't wait to see you again.

Rockingly yours,
John

Dear Palmer,
   Sorry I can't meet you at the seminar. I'll be busy that afternoon.

Yours truly,
Sam

"I don't believe this!" Palmer moaned, wadding her letter into a ball and dropping it into the wastebasket beside the desk. "I'm the only one who signed up for this stupid lecture who'll be sitting alone."

"You can sit with Mars and me," Shanon offered softly.

"Won't *that* be fun?" Palmer said, plopping onto the bed and rolling her eyes.

"That's really the pits," Amy said sympathetically. "Maybe we should all back out of the seminar."

Shanon lowered her eyes. She'd really been looking forward to seeing Mars again. "I don't think that's necessary," she mumbled. "Do you, Lisa?"

"No. There must be some way to work this out for Palmer," Lisa said thoughtfully.

"Don't worry about me!" Palmer exclaimed, bouncing back from her momentary fit of disappointment. "I don't know what's keeping Sam busy Thursday afternoon, but I'm sure if it was something he could get out of—like a dumb old baseball practice—he would."

Lisa looked at her suitemate and nodded. It would be hard to imagine any boy passing up a chance to spend time with Palmer. "Still," she began hesitantly, "don't you think it's strange that Sam didn't suggest an alternate plan to meet with you, just for a minute or two? Like, while he's on his way to whatever class he has that's tying him up?"

Palmer shook her head. "Not at all. A big shot like Sam? He's probably got tons of stuff scheduled between his classes. But I'm not giving up."

"You aren't?" Amy asked, sounding somewhat surprised.

"Definitely not." Palmer tossed her head. "The seminar is at Ardsley, right?" The other three girls nodded. "Well, how hard can it be to track Sam down there?"

"I don't know, Palmer," Lisa said. "I doubt we'll be allowed to go wandering around the campus."

Palmer gave a long sigh and smiled as she fell back onto

her bed, sending stuffed animals flying in every direction. "I guess you've just never heard of fate. Sam and I . . . our paths were destined to cross."

"How romantic," Shanon whispered dreamily.

"I think I'm going to be sick," said Amy, but she gave her roommate a friendly grin, glad to see her in a good mood again.

Lisa chewed her thumbnail and stared at the crumpled letter in the wastebasket. "I hope you do run into him. There's just something strange about his note. I still don't understand why he didn't suggest another meeting time or place instead of just letting it drop."

"Don't be such a downer, Lisa!" Palmer said. "All I really have to worry about now is what to wear for my first date with Sam." She turned toward her bedroom.

"Hey, I got another letter," Shanon cried happily.

Palmer spun around to stare at her in disbelief. "Mars wrote twice?"

"No. This one is from Petra at the Brighton School." Palmer snickered. "Our own little Hemingway."

"Don't be so sarcastic, Palmer. Just the fact that she wrote to me is a big deal for her." Shanon tore open the flap. "Listen to this—"

Dear Shanon,
I luve you very, very, very mutch. I am glad you are my frend.

OXOXOXOXOXOX,
Petra

28

"Oh, that's sweet," Lisa said.

"That's really impressive," Palmer commented sarcastically, looking over Shanon's shoulder at the letter. "Only two sentences, and she spelled three words wrong."

Amy shook her head. "You just don't get it, Palmer. This shows that Petra's learning from Shanon."

"When I started working with her, she wouldn't even write one word, she was so afraid of making mistakes. The program is really working!"

Palmer laughed. "That's the dumbest thing I've ever heard."

The other girls sat in silence as she walked out of the room.

"Sometimes," Lisa muttered under her breath, "I wonder why we even try to be nice to her."

CHAPTER FOUR

———◆———

The eight girls who had signed up for the geology seminar gathered outside the Alma van. Maggie Grayson was supposed to be driving them over to Ardsley. But when they climbed in, they found Dan Griffith, the handsome English teacher, sitting in the driver's seat.

Lisa and Shanon exchanged glances, while Amy tried unsuccessfully to smother a giggle. All the Foxes were convinced that the relationship between the two attractive young faculty members was more than just friendship. In fact, they were pretty sure it was love!

"Miss Grayson will be right along," Mr. Griffith announced. "She's picking up a batch of work sheets at Booth Hall."

"Work sheets?" Amy asked.

"Well, this *is* supposed to be a learning experience," he said, his eyes twinkling. "You Foxes wouldn't have any other reason for attending a seminar at Ardsley, would you?"

Shanon felt herself flush bright red. Lisa bit her lip nervously and stared out the window.

"Well," Amy stammered, "I—we—that is—"

Amy was saved by the breathless arrival of Maggie Grayson. "Sorry I'm late," she said. "Are we all here?"

"Present and accounted for," Mr. Griffith said, giving her a little salute.

Lisa nudged Shanon. "Isn't that cute? Look how she's blushing."

"Do you think they're in love?" Shanon whispered.

"Of course," Lisa hissed. "I wonder if they're going to get married."

"What's that?" Amy interrupted, leaning forward from the seat behind Shanon and Lisa. "Who's getting married?"

"Shh!" Lisa warned as Maggie Grayson turned around and began counting heads to be sure everyone was on board.

The girls sat in silence until Miss Grayson turned around again and Mr. Griffith started up the van.

"Who's getting married?" Amy repeated. "Them?"

"I don't know," Lisa said. She spun around on her seat to face the rear of the bus. Palmer was gazing out the window with a faraway expression in her eyes. But Amy and Shanon were giving Lisa their full attention. "I just think it would be so romantic," Lisa whispered. "They make such a good-looking couple."

Shanon let out a soft sigh. "They sure do."

Just then, the Ardsley campus came into view and the Foxes' thoughts all turned to their *own* romances. Lisa pulled a comb from her purse and quickly ran it through her long, dark hair. Amy took out a tiny folding mirror and put on a little pink lipstick she hoped wouldn't be too obvious. Rules against makeup for Alma Stephens girls were pretty strict.

As soon as the van rolled to a stop in front of the administration building, Shanon stood up in the aisle and began tugging on her skirt where she'd been sitting on it. "Do I look all right?" she asked.

"You look fine," Palmer said. "Quit fussing and let's get moving. I don't know about you three, but I'm not keeping *my* date waiting."

No one dared point out that Palmer's date was the only one who *wouldn't* be waiting for her.

"It's a short walk from here to Formby Hall where Dr. Kinsington is giving his lecture," Miss Grayson announced. "We're lucky it's such a nice day. Dan, why don't you lead the way. I'll lock the van and follow along."

"Fine with me," he said, beaming at her.

Amy raised one eyebrow and Lisa smiled slyly.

With a determined set to her shoulders, Palmer marched down the sidewalk. Ignoring everyone else, she stared across the grassy quad that separated the Ardsley buildings. Boys carrying books and notebooks walked in small groups to and from their classes.

"I feel so sorry for her," Shanon said.

"Don't waste your sympathy," Lisa told her friend. "Knowing Palmer, she'll track Sam down and set up a date with him before you even *see* Mars."

Amy giggled. "Sometimes I think she can smell a boy

32

before she can see him. She must be part bloodhound—or boyhound!"

"Let's go, girls," Miss Grayson said, shooing them on. "We don't want to be late."

Lisa, Amy, and Shanon hurried along between the huge, ancient maples, noting the pretty yellow crocuses that had poked up through the soft earth around the trees' roots. The air was sweet and warm with spring. Palmer stopped in the middle of the path, eagerly scanning the campus for a glimpse of her pen pal before hurrying to catch up with the other girls.

The group had almost reached Formby when Palmer let out a shriek. "Oh! Oh! I see someone I know! Miss Grayson, may I please just say hello?"

The pretty French teacher didn't have time to answer. Palmer was already darting across the street toward a group of boys headed in the opposite direction. One was tall and thin, with reddish-blond hair. He was wearing an Ardsley letter sweater.

The three remaining Foxes stopped to watch.

"Sam! Sam!" Palmer cried. "I'm so glad we ran into each other this way!"

"If she doesn't stop soon, she'll run *over* him," Amy pointed out.

Lisa smiled. "I told you she'd find him."

The three Ardies stopped and looked at each other. "Sam?" they asked.

Palmer screeched to a halt and stood with her hands on her hips, studying the middle boy. "You're not Sam O'Leary," she said accusingly.

"No, I'm not," he said. He looked her up and down, admiringly. "Of course, I could always change my name."

Palmer gave him a cool stare. "If you're trying to pick me up, forget it. I have a date. I just thought you were someone else."

"Sam O'Leary," repeated the middle boy thoughtfully.

Palmer nodded. "You probably know him. He's almost famous. He has his own rock band, and he's into all sorts of sports."

The three boys looked at each other. "O'Leary," repeated the one on the left.

"That's right," Palmer said proudly. "Sam O'Leary. He's lead guitarist and sometimes plays the drums for The Fantasy, his band."

"I think I've heard of The Fantasy," one of the boys said slowly. "Or some band that sounds like that anyway."

"I don't know anyone named O'Leary," the redhead said to Palmer. "Sorry."

"Well, I'm sure he doesn't know *you* either," Palmer huffed. "Imagine, not knowing one of the most popular boys in school!" She turned and crossed the street to rejoin her suitemates and Miss Grayson, who'd been watching from a distance. Because they couldn't hear the conversation, they could only guess what had been said. But it was clear that Palmer was very excited about the meeting. When she joined the others, her face was pink and her eyes were flashing.

"He's cute," Shanon said.

"Are you going to meet him later?" Amy whispered in Palmer's ear.

34

"That's *my* business," Palmer muttered and walked away from the group, straight into the building.

"What's with her?" Amy asked.

"I don't think the day is working out quite the way she'd planned," Lisa said. "I'll try to talk to her."

In the lobby, she caught up with Palmer, who was gulping water at the fountain.

"That wasn't Sam," Lisa guessed.

Palmer straightened up, wiping her lips. "No, it wasn't. And those jerks didn't even know him!"

"Ardsley is a pretty big school," Lisa said. "We don't know everyone at our own school."

"Not everyone is *worth* knowing," Palmer pronounced. "But Sam is the kind of boy everyone would know."

"Maybe they're new here," Lisa tried again. "Let's go find Rob. He and Mars and John are sure to know Sam. They might even be able to tell us where he is right now."

Palmer's eyes lit up. "That's a great idea." She grabbed Lisa's hand and dragged her into the auditorium, where the rest of the group had disappeared seconds earlier.

Lisa spotted Rob Williams right away. He, Mars, and John were sitting near the back of the room, even though there were plenty of vacant seats up front. They'd spaced themselves out, leaving a place for each of their pen pals. Lisa's heart skipped a beat. For the next few hours, she'd be able to sit right next to Rob.

Of course, they'd have to sort of pay attention to Dr. Kinsington, too. When his lecture was over, each of the girls was supposed to fill out a questionnaire based on what she'd learned. In the meantime, though, they could still whisper and pass notes—which was a whole lot better than long-distance letter writing when you couldn't even see the person you were communicating with.

Lisa sat down on one side of Rob, Palmer on the other. He looked surprised and grinned at them. "Do I get two pen pals today?"

Lisa elbowed him in the ribs. "No, silly. Palmer needs some information about one of your fellow Ardies."

"Sam O'Leary," Palmer whispered in Rob's ear, as a distinguished-looking, gray-haired man stepped up to the podium in front of the auditorium. "He plays on the Ardsley lacrosse team, and he swims and skis for your squads, too."

Rob frowned. "We don't have a ski team."

Palmer gave Lisa a confused look.

"He didn't say that he was on a team," Lisa pointed out. "He just said he liked to ski."

"Right," Palmer agreed quickly. "He's mostly a musician, with his own band. He probably performed at your dances, until he got famous and they couldn't afford him anymore."

Rob thought for a minute. Then he leaned over and said something to one of his own suitemates, Arthur "Mars" Martinez.

Shanon's pen pal stared at Palmer for a minute. "Are you sure you got his name right? I . . . um . . . I don't remember running into any O'Leary lately."

"I don't believe this," Palmer fumed. "You guys are putting me on. This is a joke, right?"

"Wait a minute." Lisa quickly scooted down the row

36

and sat beside John Adams. "John, this is really important. Think hard. Have you ever heard of a guy named Sam O'Leary at Ardsley?"

John smiled at her. "Who's he—Palmer's new pen pal?"

"Yes," Amy said. "Thank heavens she found one. She was driving us all crazy after the Simmie fiasco."

"And now she's driving us all crazy by bragging about her new pen pal, Sam," Lisa added. "But their first meeting, today, fell through. So, do you know him?"

John's dark brown eyes narrowed in concentration. "Sorry, Lisa," he said. "I'm afraid I never heard of the guy."

CHAPTER FIVE

———◆———

Palmer ran up the stairway to Suite 3-D. Lisa and the other girls took their time on the stairs, not wanting to get too close to their furious roommate. A door slammed. Palmer's bedroom door.

"It's really strange," Shanon whispered as they entered the suite. "Imagine, none of our pen pals know anything about Sam O'Leary."

"It's still possible that they just don't know him. He might be an upperclassman," Amy suggested. "Some of the older guys keep pretty much to themselves."

"Maybe," Shanon said thoughtfully.

Amy sighed. "I wish we'd had more time to talk with the boys. I could have screamed when Dr. Kinsington made us all move down to the front."

Lisa let out a long, wistful breath. Rob had even held her hand, before they'd been forced to change seats. She would have liked for the afternoon to last forever.

Unfortunately, it probably *had* seemed like an eternity to

poor Palmer, who'd just scrunched up in her seat and suffered through the entire lecture in morbid silence.

Lisa eyed Palmer's door. She thought she heard a soft snuffle from behind it. Was Palmer crying?

"We've got to do something," she said at last. "Either someone is playing a mean joke on Palmer, or there's been a terrible mix-up."

"What do you think we should do?" Shanon asked.

"I'm going to get hold of Rob and ask him some of the questions I should have asked back at Ardsley."

"But that will take days," Amy objected. "Maybe a week by mail."

"I know. So I'll just have to call him."

"On the phone?" Shanon gasped. "You're going to call a *boy* on the phone?"

Lisa smiled. "What's wrong with that? Rob and I are friends. I'm sure if he needed to find out something very important, and he thought I might help, he'd call me."

"Yeah, but ..." Shanon giggled. "I suppose you're right. You're just braver than I am."

"The real problem is finding a free telephone," Amy said logically. "The pay phone down the hall is always busy. And the one in the basement is almost as bad, plus it's cold and kind of creepy down there."

"I'll just have to get in line right away," Lisa said.

"Wait!" Amy put out a hand. "You'll miss dinner."

Although she knew the line would be twice as long after dinner, Lisa had to admit that her stomach felt pretty empty. And tonight was Italian night. One of her favorite meals was spaghetti and meatballs with crunchy garlic bread. She could eat a ton of the stuff. "This is an emergency," she said firmly. "I'll just have to sacrifice one meal for the good of the cause."

"You're a very loyal Fox," Shanon said, giving her roommate a hug. "I hope Palmer appreciates you some-day."

"I second that," Amy echoed.

"See you later," Lisa called over one shoulder, as she headed out the door.

Amy looked at Shanon. "Come on, we might as well go have supper. I'll bet Palmer won't be eating tonight either."

"I'm going to feel awfully guilty pigging out on pasta while she and Lisa go hungry," Shanon admitted.

"Me too." Then Amy stopped and stared at Shanon, her dark eyes shining. "But maybe they won't have to."

"What do you mean?" Shanon asked curiously.

"Come on. You'll see."

The two girls raced to the dining room. Mrs. Worth had already served platefuls of steaming pasta to a dozen girls who were now scattered around the cheerful room at various tables.

When Amy's turn in line came, she stepped up to the glass panel and smiled sweetly at the roly-poly English-woman. "Good evening, Mrs. Bu—I mean Mrs. Worth," she said. In private, the girls called the Alma cook Mrs. Butter, after a pancake syrup—because she was so sweet and such a softie—and sometimes it was hard not to slip in public.

"Good evening to you, love," the cook said merrily. "You look ready for a nice, hearty meal."

"Well," Amy said, dimming her smile a fraction. "I'll certainly try to eat a little bit."

"A little bit?" Mrs. Worth looked from Amy to Shanon and back again to the slender girl in the long black and red striped T-shirt dress. "You're just about skin and bones now, dearie. You'd better do better than that."

"Oh, I usually do," Amy insisted—which was true, especially when it came to pasta. "But I'm not feeling very well tonight. Neither is Shanon."

"I'm not?" Amy gave Shanon a sharp look. "No, of course not," Shanon said quickly. "I'm feeling terrible, actually."

"You poor little things," Mrs. Worth cooed. "Are you sick?"

Amy nodded. "At least we were able to come down to supper. Palmer and Lisa are still upstairs."

"What? They're not eating tonight?"

"I'm sure they'll feel better in the morning," Shanon put in. She didn't want the cook to think there was anything seriously wrong with them. She might insist that they all report to the school nurse's office.

Amy glanced at her suitemate approvingly. "Maybe after a short nap they'll be able to eat and—" She broke off suddenly, as if she'd only just thought of something. "Oh, but by then the dining room will be closed. That's too bad." She turned to Shanon. "I guess we should have woken them up."

41

Shanon nodded solemnly.

For a moment, the motherly cook looked alarmed. Then her round, pink face brightened. "I have an idea. You girls sit down and enjoy your dinner. When you're finished, come back to the kitchen. I'll have two hot plates of spaghetti for Palmer and Lisa—all wrapped up in foil. They should stay nice and toasty for at least an hour."

"Oh, thank you," Amy said, beaming. "By then, I'm sure they'll be awake and have their appetites back."

"Now, that's all right," Mrs. Worth said, obviously pleased with herself. "You just concentrate on eating well, so you'll get better fast, too."

Amy shot Shanon a triumphant look as they took their seats at the Foxes' usual center table.

Lisa didn't reach the front of the telephone line for almost forty-five minutes. She was more nervous about making the call than she'd let on to her friends. She didn't want Rob to think she was chasing him.

She dialed Ardsley's number, then asked for the extension in Rob's dorm. The phone rang eight times before someone answered.

"Yeah?" an unfamiliar boy's voice said.

"Um," Lisa said uneasily. "I'm trying to reach Rob Williams."

"Most everyone's at dinner now," the voice told her. It sounded as if the boy had something in his mouth and was chewing between words.

42

"I'm sorry," Lisa murmured, "but this is pretty important. Do you think you could find him?"

She was afraid that if she gave up her place in line, Fox Hall's dining room would empty and there'd be a rush for the phone. Then she'd never get through.

"I'll try," he promised.

As soon as he left, another voice came on the line. "Hi!"

Lisa jumped. "Hi," she replied automatically. "Rob?"

"No. Who's this?"

"This is Lisa."

"Great. This is Mark. So what do you want to talk about, Lisa?"

"I, um . . ." She wasn't sure what to do now. Whoever had first answered the phone had gone off to find Rob. If she hung up, she'd miss him. She supposed she'd better keep talking. "I was waiting for Rob Williams."

"Oh, him. He's not so great. Girls tell me I'm a super hunk, though. I'm almost six feet tall, and I'm a fifth-former."

She laughed. "Oh, really."

"Yeah, really. So, Lisa, where are you? Are you a local girl? Or do you go to Brier Hall or Alma Stephens or what?"

Lisa was tempted to make up a creative story about how she was calling from California or Texas or someplace far away. Something really wild to match the lines the mysterious boy on the other end was feeding her.

Then she heard a commotion over the wire.

"Hand it over, Romeo," a voice demanded. "She called to talk to me."

"Hey, Williams, be a sport."

"No way. Get lost." It was Rob's voice. "Lisa? You there? It's me."

"Hi," she said brightly, pleased that he'd sounded so possessive. Imagine, two boys fighting over her! But of course she only cared about Rob. "I'm sorry if I interrupted your dinner."

"You didn't. I was already finished. I was just surprised to get a call from you—and happy," he added quickly.

Lisa cupped the receiver with one hand so she could lower her voice. There were three girls waiting behind her, and she didn't want them telling the whole dorm every word she had to say to Rob. "I need to find out a little more about Sam O'Leary."

"I already told you everything I could," Rob said.

"I know. But Palmer has been getting letters from him—or someone who goes by his name. And they've got the Ardsley postmark on them."

"That's weird."

"So, I was wondering—why did John sound so sure of himself when he said there was no one at Ardsley named Sam O'Leary?"

"Because," Rob said, "John's the chairman of the Ardsley Social Committee. He knows everyone in this school."

"Everyone?" Lisa said skeptically.

"Just about," Rob insisted.

"Oh," Lisa said, disappointed. "But if there is no Sam, who's been writing to Palmer?"

"Someone with another name?" Rob suggested.

"But why? Why answer the ad under a false name?"

"I don't know," Rob admitted. "Some guys have a lousy sense of humor. Some guys you just can't figure, you know?"

A warning shiver ran down Lisa's spine. "Oh, no," she breathed. "You don't think Simmie could be behind this, do you?"

Rob hesitated. "I don't know. I haven't seen much of him lately. Last I knew, he was madly in love with a new girl, someone local."

"Figures," Lisa said. "Word's gotten around at Alma Stephens. Almost every girl here has heard what a rat he is. I don't think he'd get a date here."

"Serves him right," Rob said stiffly.

"But if it's not Simmie, who is it?" Lisa repeated.

"You'll probably never know. My advice to Palmer is, she should throw out this guy's letters and start all over with another pen pal. Tell her to forget about Sam."

"Surprise!" Amy and Shanon shouted as Lisa came through the door to the suite.

Lisa grinned when she saw the plate piled high with spaghetti, topped with four huge meatballs, steaming tomato sauce, and parmesan cheese.

"I'm starving!" she gasped. "How did you get this?"

"Let's just say Mrs. Butter is a real softie," Amy said, rocking back on her heels. "We got some for Palmer, too, and took it in to her."

"How is she?" Lisa asked, sitting on the floor in front of the coffee table. She didn't want to risk spilling sauce on the pink loveseat.

Amy just shook her head.

"I've never seen her this down," Shanon whispered.

Just then the bedroom door opened. Palmer stepped out, holding her plate. "I can't eat in bed," she mumbled. "I've lost the knack."

Lisa smiled at their friend, guessing it was the need for company that had really brought her out of her room. "Here," she said, patting the bare floor. "Pull up a seat."

Palmer didn't even crack a tiny smile, but she did sit down and try a bite of pasta. Her eyes, Lisa noted sadly, were red and swollen, as if she'd been crying.

"Palmer," she said, "don't worry. There are other boys for you."

"*Lots* of other boys," Shanon added. "You're so beautiful. Everyone loves you."

That wasn't precisely true, but neither Lisa nor Amy corrected Shanon. Palmer had her faults, but none of them liked seeing her so unhappy.

Palmer ate without speaking. For a long while, the suite was dismally quiet.

"Listen," Amy finally said, "we'll run another ad for you. We'll make it irresistible. You can choose someone new. Someone rich and interesting, just the type you like."

"The type I like is Sam," Palmer said sadly.

"I think you'd be better off forgetting about Sam," Lisa said diplomatically.

"What do *you* know?" Palmer snapped, waving her fork

46

in Lisa's direction. A big, fat meatball rolled across the floor, leaving a sticky orange trail. "First you talk me into this ridiculous pen pal scheme of yours to meet boys, and I wind up with that nerd, John Adams." She looked directly at Amy. "And then someone goes and steals him from me."

Amy rolled her eyes. "That's not how it happened, Palmer, and you know it."

"Palmer, that isn't fair," Shanon chimed in. "You know that Amy was Simmie's pen pal. It was only after you stole Simmie from her and dumped poor John that she started writing to him."

"Whatever," grumbled Palmer.

"She's just upset," Shanon said to Amy, trying to make peace.

"That's no excuse for lying," Amy insisted.

"I know, I know." Shanon's head was starting to pound. "The point is, finding nice boys has worked for the three of us. It will work for you, too, Palmer."

"Just give it another chance," Lisa begged.

Palmer lifted her perfect chin and straightened her back determinedly. "No way. I wouldn't try your stupid pen pal idea again if it was the only way on earth to meet a boy!"

CHAPTER SIX

On the following Monday, Shanon arrived early at the *Ledger* office. It had been a long weekend for everyone in Suite 3-D. Palmer's misery seemed to be rubbing off on all of them.

Shanon had decided to escape and get an early start on her day and the new week. On the way to the office, she stopped off at Booth Hall to pick up her mail. The 3-D box was crammed full with envelopes. Shanon took out the whole stack and quickly flipped through them.

"Oh, wow!" she squealed when she saw a letter addressed to her and recognized Mars's handwriting.

Dear Shanon,

It was fun seeing you at that seminar, although we didn't get much time to talk. Some of the stuff about volcanoes and lava and pumice (remember, that's the volcanic rock that floats) was really neat. Thanks for inviting me.

Now, I'm inviting you to something. The Big Mix at
Ardsley is coming up. Will you be my date?

Sincerely,
Mars

"Hi, Shanon. What's that you're reading?"

Shanon looked up to find Kate Majors standing beside her.

"A letter from Mars, my pen pal," she said, smiling.

"That's great," Kate said. "It looks like all your suite-mates got letters."

"Let's see," said Shanon, checking out the envelopes again. "Here's one for Amy."

"That's a neat stamp," Kate commented, looking over Shanon's shoulder.

Shanon studied the colorful postage stamp, then the return address. "It's from Amy's old friend in Australia, Evon."

"I'd love to have a pen pal from the other side of the world," Kate said wistfully.

"Are you still writing to Reggie McGreevy?" Shanon asked.

"No, well, yeah, I guess so. I wrote him last Wednesday." Kate fiddled with the ribbon around her flyaway ponytail.

Shanon calculated on her fingers. "That means he got it Friday. He probably wouldn't have had time to get a letter back to you. And besides, Lisa says he's not very good about writing letters."

"He's pretty good with me," Kate said, blushing.

Shanon smiled. "You must bring out another side of him, I guess. Maybe you'll get something tomorrow."

The two girls left Booth Hall together and headed toward the *Ledger* office. They worked there for an hour and then Shanon returned to the suite to pick up her books.

As she'd expected, the other girls had already left for their first class of the morning. Shanon laid the Ardsley letters on the coffee table and started out the door, then changed her mind. It would probably be kinder not to leave them lying around where Palmer might come across them. Now that she no longer had a pen pal, the mere sight of mail was apt to depress her.

By noon, Shanon still hadn't bumped into any of her suitemates. But she spotted Lisa and Amy at the end of the dining-room line.

"Isn't it absolutely beautiful outside!" Amy exclaimed when Shanon joined them.

"It must be seventy degrees out," Shanon said.

"Warmer, in the sun," Lisa added.

Shanon reached into her bookbag. "Here. We all got mail today. All except Palmer, that is."

The girls each accepted their envelopes with a guilty glance around the room. "We always open our mail together," Amy said. "What do we do now?"

"I don't know." Shanon stared at her toes. "But I have a confession to make—I already opened mine. I thought it would be best, you know, so Palmer's feelings don't get hurt."

50

"You're probably right," Lisa said as the line inched forward. She rose on tiptoe to get a look at the choices for lunch.

Mrs. Worth saw her and said, "Hello, Lisa. Glad to see you up and about again. Can I interest you in a nice hearty bowl of beef stew?"

Lisa wrinkled her nose. "Many more bowls of your stew, and I'll look like a side of beef myself! Besides, it's so warm out today. I feel like something lighter."

"Me, too," said Shanon.

"I could eat anything, just as long as it's fast," Amy put in.

"Well, I have a lovely salad with strips of cheese and turkey and ham on top. You may even take it outside on the quad to eat, as long as you pick up after yourselves when you're done."

"Oh, that sounds great!" Lisa helped herself to a large bowlful of greens and tomato and cucumber along with a generous variety of toppings.

"I thought you weren't very hungry," Amy said.

"I wasn't," Lisa admitted. "But it looks so good." She smothered her entire salad with Russian dressing.

Outside, the three girls found a graceful old maple tree to sit beneath. Lisa stuck her bare legs out to catch some rays.

"Better take off your shoes and socks, or you'll get a white line," Amy advised her.

"Who cares? No one sees my feet anyway," Lisa said, but she compromised by rolling her socks down. "All right, who starts first?"

51

"Why can't we all eat at the same time?" Amy asked, giving her a strange look.

"Not the food, Amy," Lisa groaned. "The mail. We should read our letters before Palmer shows up. I know, to start off, you can read Evon's letter to us. Then Shanon can read hers from Mars."

Amy grinned. "Okay. But I have to get some food in me first. Otherwise, I'm going to pass out from hunger."

After Amy had picked the cheese strips off her salad, her favorite part, she tore open Evon's letter.

Dear Amy,

Thanks for letting me visit you at Alma. I had a super time, and I loved meeting your roomies. Say hi to them for me!

Winter is almost here, Down Under, and just thinking about it makes me so sad. I spent nearly the whole summer at the beach! We swam and surfed and played volleyball. I had three bathing suits (one of them was the hottest bikini I've ever owned—tiger stripes—you'd have loved it!). But none of them ever got a chance to dry out because I swam constantly. The only thing that makes it easier for me to stand summer's loss is knowing that it's heading your way. Hope you enjoy it as much as I did.

Missing you,
Evon

"It's so strange to think of it being winter in Australia when it's summer here," Shanon said. "I really liked

Evon—I hope she comes back again someday."

"Maybe she will," Amy said. "There's always a chance her father might come to the United States on another business trip. If he does, I bet Evon will talk him into bringing her along. She's a genius at getting what she wants."

Lisa laughed. "Like how?"

"Well," Amy began, warming to the subject, "she told me what happened a few years ago when she wanted to go to this rock concert. Elton John. Evon just loves him. Anyway, she asked her dad to get her a ticket since he worked right downtown. But he told her she was too young to go to a rock concert—that it was too wild a crowd."

"They do get pretty crazy sometimes," Lisa commented. She'd never actually been to a rock concert, but she'd seen news clips of some and, of course, loads of videos.

"Yes," said Shanon, who hadn't been to a rock concert either, "and parents get awfully nervous about crowds. So, what did Evon do?"

"Welllll," Amy continued, her eyes bright, "her dad is totally into education. You know, pushing her grades and all. So she went to her language arts teacher and asked if she could do a special report for extra credit—"

"Don't tell me, I can guess!" Lisa squealed. "She told her she would interview Elton John!"

"Oh, no!" gasped Shanon.

"It's true," Amy assured them. "Since it was an official school assignment, her father bought two tickets—one for her and one for her older sister. The night of the concert, they hung around outside the stage door before and after the show."

"Did she get to see Elton John up close?" Lisa asked, unable to wait for Amy to finish. "Did Evon interview him?"

Amy shook her head. "No. I guess she realized that her chances weren't real good. I mean, people make up all sorts of crazy stories to get into a star's dressing room."

"The important thing," Shanon pointed out, "is that she got to go to the concert."

"Right," Amy agreed. "*And,* the funny thing is, while she was hanging out, hoping to meet Elton, Evon interviewed his chauffeur. She got some really interesting facts about his tour, and she turned them into a super report. Her teacher gave her an 'A' on it."

"Wow!" Shanon breathed. "She really is a genius. Now, do you want to hear my letter?"

"Sure," Lisa said, "go ahead and read it to us."

Shanon did, and the other girls gasped when she got to the part about the mixer.

"I hope John invited me, too!" Amy cried. "Can I read mine next?"

"Sure," Lisa said, taking another crunchy bite of salad.

Dear Amy,
Knowing how much you like music, I figured you'd want to go to the next Ardsley dance. This one should be really great. There's a super band playing. Would you like to go with me? Please write to give me your answer.

Also, would you give Palmer a message for me? Tell her I'm sorry that things aren't working out for her. I think she's not such a bad person. I've talked to Rob and Mars about an idea of mine. If you think it might make her feel better, the three of us could get together and write her a letter. You know, just as friends, so she wouldn't feel left out.

Do you think she'd like that?

> *Sincerely,*
> *John*

"Isn't that sweet?" Amy asked, still staring starry-eyed at the letter.

"Isn't that obnoxious?" a chilly voice chimed in.

The girls twisted around and saw Palmer leaning against the tree trunk.

"The boys are just trying to be nice."

"Nice my foot," sniffed Palmer, two bright pink spots appearing on her cheeks. "For all we know, they could be the ones behind this whole mess."

"How can you even suggest that?" Lisa demanded. "All three of them are completely trustworthy."

"They don't like me. They've never liked me," Palmer insisted. "And you're all sitting around gloating over your invitations to the dance, while I . . . I . . ." Tears welled up in her pretty blue eyes as she crumpled to the ground beside Lisa. "Oh, forget it. I don't care if I never see another Ardie the rest of my life. They're all a bunch of creeps, every one of them."

Lisa put an arm around her friend. "It's all right, Palmer.

55

Things look bad now. But they're bound to pick up soon."

Palmer sniffled. "Florida boys are much more interesting anyway. I can't wait for summer vacation when I can go home."

Shanon glanced at the letter in Lisa's hand. Lisa understood the silent warning and started to put the unopened envelope in her purse.

"Oh, go ahead," Palmer said. "You might as well open yours, too. It won't make a bit of difference anyway."

"You're sure?" Lisa asked.

"Sure. Why not?"

Lisa opened Rob's envelope and started to pull out the letter. But before she could unfold it, a scrap of paper slid into her lap.

"What's that?" Amy asked.

"I don't know. It looks like a page torn out of a newspaper."

"It's a photograph of a chess match," Amy said, peering over Lisa's shoulder.

Shanon and Palmer moved closer to take a look too.

They all must have seen the caption at the same time.

"Oh, no," Shanon breathed, just as Lisa's fingers tightened on the scrap.

Palmer drew a sharp breath. "That's *him!* Oh, my gosh, that's Sam. You can't mistake him in that photo, and look what it says underneath."

"Sam O'Leary, representing Ardsley Academy against Phillips-Exeter in the Fall Chess Meet," Amy said in a soft voice.

"Read Rob's letter," Palmer ordered haughtily.

Lisa unfolded the white sheet of paper.

Dear Lisa,
By now you've probably heard about the dance at the academy. I'd really like you to be my date if you—

"*Not that* part!" wailed Palmer, snatching the letter out of Lisa's hands. "The explanation for this newspaper clipping!" She continued reading rapidly in Lisa's place:

. . . I found this picture and article while I was doing some research for my social studies class. Guess there really is (or was) a Sam O'Leary, after all. But I checked the class list, and he isn't on it now. Maybe someone at Ardsley knew him from first semester and decided to use his photo and name to write to Palmer. Sort of like the way crooks on TV shows use a dead person's name for a new identity. Pretty clever, in a warped sort of way. He sounds like a real loser. Like I said, Palmer would be better off forgetting about this guy. . . .

Palmer's voice faded off and she stared at the other girls in stunned silence.

"I don't believe this is happening," Shanon whispered.

Lisa gently pried the letter out of Palmer's fingers. She was afraid of the explosion that was bound to come as soon as Palmer's brain started functioning again. Mostly, she was afraid of what Palmer might do to Rob's letter in a fit of disappointment.

"This is awful," Amy breathed.

57

"Terrible," Shanon agreed, shaking her head sadly.

"Rob could be wrong, you know," Lisa suggested reasonably. "I mean, he's only guessing. All this really proves is that there once was a Sam O'Leary at Ardsley."

Palmer rose slowly to her feet. "Well," she said, tossing her blond hair back from her face, "I'll tell you one thing. Whoever this Sam O'Leary is, someone ought to teach him some manners!" Her cheeks glowed, and her lips were trembling.

"Palmer," Lisa began, wanting to comfort her. But Palmer was already marching across the quad, back toward Fox Hall.

CHAPTER SEVEN

The next afternoon the Alma girls were scheduled to tutor in Brighton again. As soon as the van pulled up in front of Fox Hall, Kate popped into Suite 3-D.

"Let's get a move on, Shanon . . . Palmer," she called.

Shanon looked up from the pink loveseat, where she'd been tying her sneakers. "I can't wait to see Petra again," she said. "Every time we meet, she surprises me with something new she's learned."

"I know what you mean," Kate replied. "I feel as if I'm really making a difference in my third-grader's life. Little Max is so adorable."

"I think he's got you wrapped around his little finger," Shanon teased. "I saw that big good-bye hug he gave you last week."

Kate grinned. "He *is* sweet." She looked around the sitting room. "Where's Palmer?"

"She was here a minute ago. I told her we'd be leaving soon." Shanon finished knotting the second lace, then walked over to the bedroom door and knocked. "Van's here," she shouted.

There was no answer.

Kate frowned. "Are you sure Palmer's in there?"

"She has to be. She didn't leave the suite." Shanon knocked harder this time.

A soft moan came through the door.

Shanon frowned anxiously. She'd been worried about Palmer all day. One moment the junior deb was on the verge of tears, the next she was strutting around, insulting everyone in the suite for no apparent reason. Shanon suspected that cutting others down was the only way Palmer believed she could build herself up, now that she'd been dumped by her pen pal—again!

Slowly, she opened the bedroom door. And there was Palmer, lying on her bed, eyes shut, knees pulled up to her stomach. Shanon ran over and knelt beside her. "What's wrong?" she asked gently.

"I feel horrible," Palmer groaned. She lifted one eyelid to peer pitifully at Kate, who stood behind Shanon. "I don't think I can even stand up."

"You seemed all right a few minutes ago," Shanon said, giving her a concerned look. "What happened?"

"I don't know. All of a sudden my stomach started to hurt so awfully. O-o-o-oh!" Palmer groaned again, clutching her abdomen.

Kate reached down and placed her hand on Palmer's forehead. "You don't feel feverish. Is it just your stomach?"

Palmer nodded. "I think I ate something that didn't agree with me. Pancakes for breakfast."

"If you drown them in syrup like the rest of the girls, it's no wonder you have a stomachache," Kate observed. "You'd better stay here and rest."

"We'll tell Miss Grayson you're sick," Shanon said sympathetically. "I hope you feel better," she murmured as she tiptoed across the room.

Palmer just squeezed her eyes shut tighter and turned her face to the wall.

A few minutes later, Shanon and Kate climbed into the waiting van. When they got to the library the small group of third-graders were already waiting in the children's room, seated in a circle on the floor. Petra immediately spotted Shanon and came hurtling toward her, springy black curls bobbing.

Shanon gave the little girl a squeeze. "How are you today?" she asked.

"I'm happy!" Petra danced around her. "Look! I brought you something."

"Oh," Shanon gasped dramatically, "I love presents."

"It's not really a present," Petra said apologetically. "It didn't cost anything. I made it."

"Just because you didn't pay money for it doesn't mean it's not a present. It's the giving that counts."

Petra beamed.

Accepting the bright red square of construction paper from the little girl, Shanon carefully unfolded it. Inside was a crayon drawing of two stick figures holding stick hands.

One was much taller than the other. They were labeled: *Petra and Shanon*. Above them was the word *FRIENDS*— and it was spelled correctly!

"What a beautiful card," Shanon said.

"Do you really, really, really like it?" Petra asked.

"I love it," Shanon said. "I think it's the nicest—"

A shrill cry pierced the library. Shanon's head shot up. On the other side of the room, Miss Grayson was talking to Gabby. Or, at least, she was trying to talk to her.

"Gabby. Gabby, listen to me," the teacher pleaded, holding the little girl's chubby hands. "Palmer's sick. She'd be here with you, if she could. I'll be your tutor today."

"I don't want you to be my tutor!" Gabby shouted. "I want Palmer!" She tugged her hands free.

"Gabby, please. You'll disturb the other children. If you don't want to work with me, you can choose someone else. Kate? Shanon? Murphy? Jennifer?"

"I want *Palmer!* Palmer, Palmer, Palmer!" Gabby shrieked, tears streaming down her flushed cheeks.

It took both Miss Grayson and the third-grade teacher who always escorted the younger students to the Brighton Project sessions to maneuver Gabby out of the room and into a hallway. They shut the door behind them, muffling only slightly Gabby's outburst.

After a while, Miss Grayson returned to the room, looking drained and worried. "This is so unfortunate," she said to no one in particular. "They were making such fine progress."

The session passed quickly. Shanon enjoyed working with Petra so much she could easily have stayed a second hour. But poor Gabby, once she was allowed to return to the room with the other children, was miserable the entire time. She sat silently in a corner, refusing even to look at her book.

Shanon felt so sorry for the little girl.

At last the tutors and their charges said good-bye and headed for the vans. Shanon and Kate sat together on the ride back to Alma.

"I hope Palmer's feeling better," Kate commented.

"Right," Shanon agreed. "I don't think Gabby could survive missing a second session with her favorite tutor."

The two girls parted ways in front of Fox Hall, Shanon rushing off to check on Palmer. She pushed open the door to 3-D and was met by a blast of rock music. Shanon stood in the doorway, trying to figure out where it was coming from. Lisa's and her door was open; it had to be Palmer's stereo turned all the way up.

Amy should be more considerate, Shanon thought. After all, Palmer wasn't feeling well.

But when Shanon stepped into the bedroom, her eyes opened wide with surprise. Lounging comfortably against a pile of pillows on her bed was Palmer, curlers in her hair, a chocolate bar in her mouth.

Shanon squinted suspiciously at her friend. "I thought you were sick!"

"Huh?" said Palmer, bobbing her head to the music.

Shanon reached over and flicked off the tape. "Sick! Ill! You were *dying* a few hours ago!"

Palmer shrugged and took another bite of the candy bar.

"You seem to have recovered nicely," Shanon continued.

63

"But are you sure you should be eating that? I don't think chocolate is very good for a stomachache."

"I'm trying to get my strength back," Palmer said, polishing off the last of the candy and licking her fingers.

"You look pretty strong to me," Shanon said wryly.

Palmer heard the doubt in her suitemate's voice. She rolled her eyes, dropping the last shreds of her act. "This tutoring business is a really stupid idea. I mean, what do I know about teaching some little kid math? I'm *terrible* at math!"

"Gabby needs you, Palmer," Shanon said. "What's *terrible* is the way you—" At the sound of the sitting-room door opening and closing, she interrupted herself in mid-sentence. "Oh, what's the use?" she said, giving Palmer a disgusted look and stalking out of the room.

Lisa and Amy were in the sitting room, having just returned from their classes. One look at Shanon's face and Lisa drew a fast breath. "What's wrong?"

"Palmer! Sometimes that girl makes me so mad!"

"What did she do now?" Amy asked.

"She pretended to be sick, to get out of working with Gabby."

"That's terrible," Lisa said just as Palmer waltzed blithely past them, picked up a *Seventeen* magazine from the table, and returned to her bedroom.

All three girls glared after her.

Shanon felt a flush of heat rise to her face. It took a lot to push Shanon over the edge. Of the four girls, she was the slowest to anger. But Palmer had gone too far this time.

Shanon took a deep breath and started to follow her.

"What are you going to do?" Lisa demanded.

"I don't know!" Shanon managed, her throat tight, before marching into Palmer's room.

Palmer was back on her bed, browsing through the magazine now. "I really wish you'd knock," she said airily when Shanon stopped at the side of her bed.

Shanon plucked the magazine out of Palmer's hands and dropped it on the bureau.

"What's *your* problem?" Palmer asked.

Lisa and Amy stood in the doorway, not sure whether to come in or not.

"You've got the worst attitude of anyone I've ever met," Shanon said shakily. "I can't believe how selfish you are!"

"Me? Selfish?" Palmer looked genuinely shocked. "I didn't do a thing. It's you three who are selfish, always gossiping about your precious pen pals, leaving me all alone."

"Don't you dare try to make us feel sorry for you." Shanon tapped her foot in warning. "Not after what you pulled today."

"So, I was sick for an hour or so." Palmer shrugged. "What's the big deal?"

"The big deal is Gabby. She was just beginning to depend on you—and you let her down."

"That little brat?" Palmer laughed, but she suddenly dropped her eyes.

"Well, that little brat seems to think you're something special," Shanon said. "When you didn't show up, Miss

Grayson offered to tutor her. Gabby threw a fit—screaming and crying. She wouldn't let anyone else in the whole Brighton Project work with her."

Palmer glanced up at Amy and Lisa, then back to Shanon. "You're kidding."

"I most certainly am not," Shanon said. "Miss Grayson even told me that Gabby's school reports show her math skills are definitely improving. And her attitude about her other subjects is better too."

Palmer stared mutely at Shanon. It was one of the rare times she could find nothing to say.

"If you pull out of the project because you're feeling sorry for yourself, Gabby's going to suffer. And that's not fair."

Palmer fiddled with the edge of her bedspread. "Who said anything about pulling out?" she mumbled. "I didn't think she even liked me. She never seems to listen to me. All she wants to do is play."

"Maybe she's just trying to get your attention," Lisa suggested. "You know, make *you* like *her*."

Palmer let out a long breath. "I never thought I could help anyone else be better at anything. I'm so awful at schoolwork—especially math."

The girls stood by in silence. Shanon felt the anger slowly drain out of her as Palmer's blue eyes met hers.

"Know what I'm going to do?" Palmer asked at last.

The others shook their heads.

"I'm going to make sure I don't miss another session with Gabby. And I'm going to work super hard to do the best I can, tutoring her. I'll even prepare little lessons—you

66

know, games that will hold her attention better so she'll learn faster."

"That's a nice idea," Lisa said, wondering if Palmer would actually follow through with it.

Shanon smiled.

"And I'm going to start doing all my own math home-work," Palmer announced grandly, "and studying for my tests ahead of time, without relying on Amy to bail me out at the last minute." She grinned, pleased with herself.

Shanon shook her head. "That I'll believe when I see it."

"Well," Palmer assured her, "from now on, you're going to see a brand-new me."

CHAPTER EIGHT

———◆———

"Time for breakfast! Rise and shine!" chirped Palmer, flinging the bed covers off her roommate.

"Leave me alone," Amy groaned, pulling the sheet back up over her head.

"Now, now. Let's not be grumpy on a beautiful morning like this." Palmer skipped out of the room, across the sitting room to the second bedroom, and pounded on the door. "Come on, you two sleepyheads. Get up!"

Lisa stared at the dial on her radio alarm. "I can't believe it. Eight o'clock."

"Isn't it Saturday?" Shanon mumbled.

"It's Saturday, Palmer. Go back to sleep!"

"Not on your life. Remember, we have a pass to go to the mall this morning. We'll shop till we drop."

"Haven't you noticed? I'm already in drop position," Lisa groaned.

"I don't think I can take any more of this cheerfulness, this good will toward men ... and girls," Shanon said from beneath her pillow. Palmer had entered the room and was pulling open the curtains. "I liked the old Palmer better."

Palmer laughed. "You can be so weird, Shanon. Now, I've already taken my shower. You go next. After everyone's dressed, we'll grab a quick breakfast and then meet Miss Grayson at the van. Okay?"

"Okay," muttered Lisa, giving way to Palmer's enthusiasm.

Lisa chose a bright purple mini-dress with turquoise tights. The dress even made her eyes look purplish in the sunlight. Over it, she wore her favorite necklace, made from her grandfather's gold pocket watch.

Shanon stood staring at the closet for a full five minutes. "My wardrobe is such a disaster," she moaned. "I don't mind wearing the same old skirts and blouses to class. Thanks to the dress code, everyone looks more or less the same there. But I never have anything even slightly cool to wear off-campus."

"You can borrow my pink jeans and beaded sweater," Palmer offered.

"For real!" Shanon gasped. She often borrowed Lisa's clothes but wouldn't have dreamed of asking Palmer to lend her a hair ribbon! The old Palmer would have been annoyed if any of the Foxes had so much as touched one of her possessions.

"Sure," Palmer said breezily. "Why not! The pants might be a little long, but I'll show you how to roll the cuffs."

"Thanks, Palmer," Shanon said quietly. It was hard to

believe. Only a week ago, she'd been ready to throw Palmer out of the suite for disappointing Gabby. But since then, Palmer had had two wonderful sessions with the little girl. And, although Palmer hadn't exactly aced her most recent math quiz, she had taken responsibility by studying for it on her own.

"Well, I'm ready," Amy said, stepping out of the bedroom.

"Wow, that's rad," Lisa proclaimed.

Amy wore cropped black pants and a black T-shirt decorated with a metallic gold tiger's-head decal. Two rows of gold bangle bracelets clinked at her wrists.

Palmer followed her into the room. She'd made a last-minute change into an aqua skirt and knit top to match her eyes.

"You look fabulous, Palmer," Lisa said. "If a dozen boys at the mall don't swarm all over you, I'll eat my barrette."

Palmer laughed. "Remember, I've sworn off boys. I can do perfectly well without them," she said with a touch of her old haughtiness.

"Yeah, sure," Lisa said. "We'll keep count of how many throw themselves at your feet."

"*And* how many you turn down," Amy said.

The mall wasn't as large as those Amy and Palmer were used to. But it was still a wonderful treat to be let loose there after spending so much time confined to the campus.

"Meet me back in the parking lot at two o'clock, sharp,"

Miss Grayson said. "I have some shopping of my own to do."

"I'll bet she's looking for a wedding gown," Shanon sang in Lisa's ear.

"Oh, maybe we should follow her!"

"Follow who?" asked Palmer.

"Never mind," Lisa said. On second thought, if Maggie Grayson was shopping for something that had to do with Dan Griffith, she wouldn't want four giggly girls tagging along.

"Where do we go first?" Amy asked, anxious to get started. "Four hours at a mall isn't much time."

Lisa laughed. "Four hours will waste me."

"Not me," Palmer bragged. "I can shop twenty-four hours straight without even getting tired."

Amy laughed. "That's our Palmer! Mega-shopper!"

The four Foxes walked from the main entrance toward a large fountain in a central courtyard. Rock music blared out of several nearby shops. The smell of popcorn, pizza, hamburgers, and fries drifted along on the gentle spring breeze.

"I'm hungry. Let's eat first," Amy said.

"We just had breakfast," Lisa reminded her. "We have plenty of time to eat. Let's walk through the whole mall first. We'll check out each store's windows to see which ones look the most interesting. Then we can vote on where to start."

"That sounds like a good idea," Amy said.

The others agreed.

They started out according to the plan. But after the first four shops, their willpower began to fade.

"Oh, the record store!" Amy cried. "I've just got to get the Bangles' new album. What if they sell them all before we get back?"

Lisa bit her lip thoughtfully. "If they have any in now, it's not likely an hour will make much difference."

"But it might," Amy said, her dark eyes fixed longingly on the window.

"Oh, why not," Palmer said at last. "Besides, I'd like to take a look around too."

They spent a half hour browsing through the CDs and tapes, checking out their favorite groups' latest posters and buttons. Amy bought her tape, and then they moved on.

"I could really use some pants and a sweater like these," Shanon said, indicating the outfit she'd borrowed from Palmer.

"I don't think you'll find anything like those here," Palmer said. "My mother got them for me at a boutique in Palm Beach."

"Oh." Shanon was disappointed. She thought the pink outfit looked really nice on her.

"Maybe we could find something similar," Lisa put in hopefully. "It wouldn't have to be exactly the same, would it, Shanon?"

"No. Just something casual but pretty. I like the beads sewn across the top. And the color's great."

"There's a shop just two doors down with pastel things in the window. Let's try there," Amy suggested.

With Palmer's expert help, Shanon was able to find a pair of pants and sweater almost the same color and style as the ones she was wearing.

"The top isn't hand-beaded," Palmer couldn't help pointing out, "but I doubt anyone would notice."

Lisa grinned. "No one but you, Palmer."

Shanon giggled. "That's all right. Thanks, Palmer. I couldn't have found my new outfit without you."

Palmer shrugged. "It wasn't anything special." But she was smiling broadly.

Next, the girls followed Lisa's craving for a chocolate milk shake to the snack shop. To keep her company, they each had a shake—but Amy and Palmer ordered vanilla, and Shanon had strawberry.

"I didn't see a single thing I really fell in love with," Palmer sighed as she finished her shake. "Nothing here is quite my style."

"Don't tell me you're going to walk away from a mall without buying *anything!*" Lisa teased.

Amy shook her head in mock disbelief. "The Palm Beach Princess's reputation will never be the same."

Palmer looked at each of them. Then she stood up decisively and tossed her paper cup in the trash. "You're absolutely right," she proclaimed. "I can't disappoint my public. I guess I'll have to *force* myself to buy that red silk blouse we saw at Gina's."

Arms linked, the four girls strolled down the walkway in the direction of Palmer's blouse. They were almost there when the super-shopper herself came to a sudden stop,

73

pulling them all to a halt outside Suzy's Shoe Emporium.

"Now that's not a bad selection of shoes," Palmer said, admiring the display of pretty high-heeled pumps.

"I love the black patent-leather ones with the thin straps," Lisa said, knowing she couldn't afford them.

"I like those too," Amy agreed. "But I'd like them better if they were higher—spikes!"

Shanon stepped closer to the window. "Those pink flats in the display near the back of the store would look wonderful with my new top and pants. Don't you think so, Palmer?"

The tall blonde moved up to the window and shielded her eyes from the glare on the glass. "I don't see them."

"Way in the back," Shanon directed. "Over by those customers and the salesman."

Palmer followed Shanon's pointing finger to a little pyramid of casual shoes beside the cashier's counter. The shoes were nice, but the salesman was what really caught her eye. He couldn't have been much older than she was—fifteen at the most. He was slim, with pale reddish-gold hair and a knock-dead smile.

"Oh, no!" Palmer gasped, clutching Shanon's arm. Her face turned pink and then paled to white.

"What's wrong?" Lisa asked, coming up behind her.

"It's . . . it's . . . h-h-him!"

"Him who?" asked Shanon, still trying to see who Palmer was talking about.

"Don't stare!" Palmer yipped. She ducked down below the level of the window, dragging Shanon with her.

Lisa and Amy squatted beside her.

74

"It's Sam, isn't it?" Lisa whispered.

"Yes . . . I don't know . . . I think so," Palmer wailed. "At least that guy looks a lot like his picture. Oh, what am I going to do? I know," she said, her voice suddenly sounding stronger, "I'm going to walk straight in there and tell him to his face what a rat he is and how much I hate him."

"What if it's not him?" Amy asked.

Shanon nodded. "You'd feel awfully dumb if it was some stranger, some other boy who didn't even know you."

"If it isn't Sam, it's his twin," Palmer declared, her cheeks flushing again.

She started to stand up, but Lisa pulled her back down. "No. There's only one thing to do. You stay here, out of sight. Shanon, make sure she doesn't move. Amy and I will check him out."

The two Foxes stood up, nonchalantly smoothing out their rumpled clothing. Then they strolled into Suzy's. Lisa walked over to the first display inside the store and picked up a pair of what happened to be men's loafers. She stared at the stitching around the toe, as if studying the workmanship.

"He's coming over," Amy whispered, her throat hoarse.

"Good."

Amy coughed nervously. "Why are you looking at men's shoes?"

Lisa started to put the loafer down, but she wasn't fast enough.

"May I help you with something?" a deep voice asked.

Lisa looked up into the lightly freckled face of the boy they'd spotted through the window. "I was . . . um . . . I was looking for a birthday present. For my father," she added.

"Oh," the boy said, smiling politely. "Well, those shoes would make a very fine gift. But it's kind of difficult buying shoes for someone else. Sometimes the fit can be a little tricky."

Amy grabbed Lisa's arm and hissed in her ear, "Why did you have to pick *men's* shoes?"

Lisa shook her off. "Well, he really needs new shoes. And I'd like to surprise him." An idea struck her. A wonderful idea! She replaced the loafer on the display table. "If they don't fit, can he exchange them for the right size?"

"Of course," said the boy. "No problem."

"Great." Lisa grinned.

"What size does he usually take?"

Lisa looked at Amy in panic. Amy shrugged. "Oh, I don't know. Maybe an eight? Or a fifteen? Something like that."

Out of the corner of her eye, Lisa saw Palmer pop up on the other side of the display window. Then Shanon's arm reached out and pulled her down again.

"If . . . if he brought them back," Lisa stammered, "could he ask for you? I mean, you know, what's your name, just in case?"

"Just tell him to ask for Sam O'Leary," the boy said with a friendly smile.

"Oh, well . . . uh, Sam, I'll tell him to ask for you."
Lisa's voice had suddenly gone squeaky with nerves. All
she wanted to do now was dash out of the store and shout
the news to Palmer.

"So, do you want the shoes?" Sam asked patiently.

"Shoes?" she echoed.

"I can give them to you in a twelve. That's about
average."

"Maybe I'd better talk it over with my friend," Lisa said,
fishing for Amy's hand as they backed away toward a
corner of the store.

"Why did you tell him you wanted to buy a pair of
men's shoes?" Amy whispered urgently. "Did you see the
price tag on those things? They're over a hundred dollars!"

"I'm not buying the shoes. I just wanted to find out his
name. And I did!" Lisa said excitedly.

Amy smiled. "You're tricky."

"Yeah. But now we've got a problem."

"Another one?"

"Definitely." Lisa glanced over her shoulder. Sam was
watching them with a puzzled expression. "Maybe we
should tell Sam that someone at Ardsley has been writing
to Palmer, using his name."

Amy thought for a moment. "You're right. If someone's
playing a mean joke on both Palmer *and* Sam, Sam ought
to be told. He's just as much a victim as Palmer."

Lisa turned around. The salesman was halfway across
the store. "Sam?" she called out.

"Yes?"

77

Even from her hiding place, Palmer heard Lisa call Sam's name . . . and heard him respond. Trembling, she slipped out of Shanon's grasp and stood up.

Just then, Sam's glance swerved toward the glass. For a moment he stared at Palmer on the other side of the window. She was so shocked, she couldn't move.

Shanon leaped up and began tugging on her arm, but Palmer just stood there. And though Lisa jumped in front of Sam, trying to block his line of sight, he was too tall and simply looked over her head.

"Palmer?" he blurted out.

CHAPTER NINE

Lisa and Amy stared at Sam, both with the same thought in mind. If he knew Palmer by sight, then he must have been the one writing to her!

Not knowing what else to do, Lisa grabbed Amy's hand, and the two girls ran out of the store.

"Wait! Hey, wait a minute!" Sam shouted from the doorway of the Shoe Emporium.

Lisa looked around. Palmer and Shanon were nowhere in sight.

"Where did they go?" Amy asked breathlessly.

"I bet I know."

They didn't stop running until they reached the snack shop. Palmer was seated at a table, her big blue eyes brimming with tears. Shanon stood helplessly over her.

"I've never been so humiliated in my life!" Palmer wailed, causing the people at several nearby tables to turn and stare. "A shoe salesman! He doesn't even go to Ardsley!"

"Oh, Palmer," Amy said, putting a comforting arm around her roommate.

"I don't get it," Shanon said.

"You're not the only one," Lisa added as she pulled up a chair and sat down. "If Sam doesn't go to Ardsley, how did he get Palmer's letters?"

"And what about the rock tape?" Amy asked.

"What about it?" said Palmer, dabbing at her eyes with a napkin.

"Did Sam really make it? I mean, he lied about going to Ardsley. Do you think he lied about the tape, too? Maybe it's some professional group."

"That's a possibility," Lisa admitted sadly. "After all, any boy could *say* he was playing guitar, or drums, or something on a tape. Who'd know?"

Palmer let out a groan of frustration and disappointment. She dropped her head onto her folded arms. "This is a nightmare," she mumbled.

Lisa glanced at Amy and Shanon. "Is there anything we can do to make you feel better, Palmer?"

"Ice cream. I'll drown my sorrows in ice cream."

"I'll buy you a cone," Shanon offered. "What flavor do you want, Palmer?"

"Make it a Super Banana Split, with everything on it."

Amy rolled her eyes as Shanon took off at a run for the ice-cream counter. "You'll explode."

"I don't care," Palmer said. "I could gain two hundred pounds. No one would notice."

"Listen," Lisa said, sitting down beside her, "any way you look at it, this was a mean trick. Sam must have had

80

help from someone at Ardsley to pull it off. Someone showed him the ad. Then they must have been picking up your letters to him."

"We'll find out who's behind this," Amy promised.

"I don't care," Palmer sniffed. "I *told* you I hate boys. All boys. I want nothing more to do with any of them. It doesn't matter where they go to school, or whether they're in a band or not, or if they have money . . . or look like gods. I'm through with them forever!"

"Palmer," Lisa said soothingly, "you don't really mean that."

Palmer's eyes sparked with blue lightning. "I most certainly do!"

The next day was Sunday—traditionally a day for sleeping late. But the sun shining through their bedroom window was so brilliant that Shanon and Lisa woke early.

"It's almost like summer," Lisa said with a sigh. "Let's get Amy and Palmer and walk down to the lake to feed the ducks."

"Great idea," Shanon said eagerly. "Mrs. Butter keeps leftover bread in the freezer. She told me the ducks like it."

"Super!" Lisa bounced out of bed and ran across the sitting room in her nightshirt. Knocking on Amy and Palmer's door, she shouted, "Hey, anyone for a walk down to the lake?"

There were footsteps on the other side of the door. Amy opened it with a sleepy smile. "Sure. Just wait till I get dressed."

"What about Palmer?" Lisa asked, peering around the

edge of the open door. All she could see was a lump in Palmer's bed. The pillow hid her head.

"I don't think she's in the mood," Amy said sadly.

Lisa sighed. "I suppose not."

Twenty minutes later, the three girls were downstairs in the kitchen. Mrs. Butter was more than happy to give them a plastic bag full of stale bread for the ducks, but she shook her head despairingly when they refused anything but croissants and juice for themselves.

As soon as they got to the lake, Amy opened the bread bag. "Doesn't look very appetizing to me," she commented, wrinkling her nose.

Lisa giggled. "You're not a duck."

The girls stood at the shore, tearing the crusts into little pieces and tossing them to the ducks. Whenever a piece of bread hit the water, there was a flurry of wings as four or five birds dove for it.

"They must really be hungry," Shanon said.

Amy held up the bag. "Hey, gang, there's plenty for everyone!"

The three Foxes laughed, enjoying the early morning sunshine, but after a while Lisa's smile faded. "It doesn't seem right, having fun like this when Palmer's so miserable."

"I know what you mean," Amy said. "She'd just begun to seem like a real friend, like one of us. She was helping Gabby so much, and taking responsibility for her own schoolwork. She even moved most of her clothes back to her own side of the closet."

"It just isn't fair," Shanon murmured.

During the next few days, Palmer's dark mood grew even more intense. On Monday, she hardly said a word to anyone. She didn't smile once all day Tuesday. And on Wednesday, she went to bed right after dinner. The girls in 3-D gave up trying to cheer her.

On Thursday afternoon, Palmer climbed into the Alma van behind Shanon and sat down glumly.

"What's in the bag?" Shanon asked, hoping to get Palmer talking on the way to their Brighton Project tutoring session.

Palmer turned to face her. "Something for Gabby."

"That's nice," Shanon said softly. "You're really starting to get through to her."

Palmer gave her a sad smile, but was silent for the rest of the trip.

At the library, Gabby greeted Palmer with a squeal and a hug. Palmer couldn't help grinning as she hugged her back. "I brought you a treat," she told Gabby.

"You did? You did?" screeched the third-grader, jumping up and down in excitement.

Palmer handed the little girl the small, brown paper sack she'd been carrying. "You can have one now and another after you complete your first five problems."

Gabby pulled a purple gummy worm out of the sack. "Ooooh, yum!" She bit off the worm's head then looked up at Palmer, her eyes bright. "What about the rest of them? Are they *all* for me?"

"Every time you get five problems right, you can have another worm."

83

By the end of the session, it was clear that the gummy-worm plan was an unqualified success. Gabby had never worked harder, and every worm was gone.

For the first time all week, Palmer felt truly happy. She couldn't wait to get back to the dorm to share her success with her roommates. But when she and Shanon walked into Suite 3-D, three letters from the Ardsley pen pals were sitting on the coffee table.

"Looks like we got mail!" Shanon couldn't stop herself from exclaiming.

Lisa and Amy glanced up from the floor, where they were stretched out studying.

"We waited for you to get back before we read them," Lisa explained.

Palmer stopped cold, just inside the door.

"Palmer," Lisa murmured, casting a worried glance in her direction. "If you like, we won't read them until later."

"Don't be childish," Palmer sniffed. "Go ahead. Read them. It won't bother me in the least."

Lisa studied Palmer's tense stance. "Are you sure you don't mind?" she persisted.

"Why should I mind?" Palmer said coolly. But as her suitemates began ripping open their letters with uncontrollable glee, she felt the glow of her victory with Gabby fading fast.

"Go ahead and read them," she said, her eyes glistening with tears. "They're probably all about that stupid dance. Well, I wouldn't go to another dumb Ardsley mixer if you paid me. I have better things to do with my time!"

"Palmer," Lisa said, "just because you don't have a date,

that doesn't mean you can't go to the mixer. You'll probably meet someone very nice there. A lot of boys would love to dance with you."

"No way," Palmer huffed. "No way. And if you three go . . . well, you can just forget about being my friends," she added, whirling around and stalking into her room.

Shanon stared dismally after her. "We've got to do something about this."

"You're right," Lisa agreed. "It's one thing for Palmer to swear off boys forever. But if we don't act fast, she'll make us lose our pen pals, too."

"The only way to help her feel better is to get to the bottom of the Sam mystery," Amy said thoughtfully. "Maybe there's something we've overlooked, some simple explanation for it all."

"I wish there was," Lisa said. She glanced hesitantly at Shanon. "This really is an emergency situation. We need help. Do you think you could reach John at the Lit. Mag?"

Shanon chewed her lip. "You mean, contact him through the computer? I don't know. Dolores has been watching the computer time pretty closely." Dolores Countee, an upperclassman at Alma, was editor-in-chief of the school newspaper. Lately, she'd been on the warpath, trying to track down unauthorized use of the computer.

Amy grimaced. "Shanon could get in big trouble if she got caught. Why don't we just try to call the boys on the third-floor phone?"

Lisa shook her head. "Easy for you to say. You didn't see how long it took me to get through to Rob. Anyway, it's not just the time. I don't want everyone in Fox Hall to know some boy has been making a fool out of poor Palmer. She's been humiliated enough as it is."

Shanon nodded. "Lisa's right. We have to do this secretly. But there's got to be another way to reach the boys quickly. The rules about unauthorized use of the computer are very serious. If anyone got caught . . ." Shanon's face paled at the mere thought.

Lisa nodded. "I know. But Palmer needs our help. And there is no other way. Please, Shanon . . .? You've got to do it. You're the only one who knows how to use the computer."

Shanon took a deep breath. She *never* broke rules. Well, hardly ever!

"All right," she finally said weakly. "The Journalism Club meets at four on Friday. I'll try to reach John after my last class tomorrow."

CHAPTER TEN

As Shanon had hoped, the *Ledger* office was deserted when she arrived after her math class the next day. Laying her bookbag on the floor beside a chair, she flicked on the computer and modem, then nervously entered her ID number and the code that would allow her access to special services.

She waited impatiently, casting a worried look over her shoulder at the door. Everything was quiet, except for the computer's low hum. She couldn't hear anyone passing by in the hall, but she was still uneasy.

Finally, she completed the sequence of commands to call up the Journalism Club program. She was overjoyed to see John's ID number on the screen—letting her know he was online too.

"Good," she whispered.

Shanon typed: /SEN99 HI, JOHN. SHANON HERE. /GA

After a brief pause, a return message appeared on her

screen: OKAY. WHAT'S UP, SHANON? /GA

Her fingers flying across the keyboard now, Shanon briefly outlined the latest developments in the Sam O'Leary mystery and begged John and his roommates to help the Foxes get to the bottom of it.

There was a long pause. Shanon's eyes darted to the office door again. What was taking John so long? Why didn't he just answer?

At last, John's reply flickered across her screen: OKAY. I CALLED THE OTHERS. MARS FINALLY ADMITS HE KNOWS SAM O'LEARY, AND THAT HE REALLY IS A ROCK SINGER. SAM DROPPED OUT OF ARDS-LEY AFTER LAST SEMESTER. GOES TO PUBLIC HIGH SCHOOL IN BRIGHTON. WILL BE AT DANCE TOMORROW NIGHT. /GA

Shanon stared at the screen in disbelief. Mars knew all along? How could that be?

Shanon raised her hands again to the keyboard. But before she could ask John any more questions, another hand reached over her shoulder and hit the power button on the computer. The screen went blank.

"Oh!" Shanon cried. And with a horrible sinking feeling in the pit of her stomach, she slowly turned around.

"What do you think you're doing?" Dolores Countee demanded shrilly, arms crossed over her chest.

Shanon's hands shook as she drew them away from the keyboard. "I was . . . I was just . . . "

"Don't tell me you were working on a story. I haven't assigned any for the next issue."

"I know," Shanon admitted, unable to lie.

"Who were you online with?"

Shanon was silent.

Dolores glared at her. "I guess it doesn't matter if you tell me or not. I'm sure I can guess. You were talking to your Ardsley pen pal. Don't you know personal use of the computer is strictly against the rules?"

"Yes," Shanon said bravely. "I know."

"Then I have no choice but to restrict you from using the computers."

"I understand," Shanon said meekly. She felt as if she were going to be sick.

"*And*," Dolores added for good measure, "as of this moment, you are officially suspended from working on *The Ledger*."

Horrified, Shanon stared at Dolores. "Suspended?"

"At least until I can meet with Miss Pryn. We'll let *her* decide your *real* punishment!"

Lisa glanced up as Shanon walked into the suite. "What happened to you?" she asked. "You look as if you've seen a ghost."

"Worse," Shanon answered shakily. "Dolores Countee saw *me!* She caught me at the computer."

Amy put down the novel she'd been reading for a book report. "Oh, no!"

"Oh, yes." Shanon tossed her bookbag on the floor. "She caught me on the computer, before John could sign off. She's going to report me to Miss Pryn."

Lisa groaned. "I'm so sorry, Shanon. This is all my fault. I made you do it."

"No, you didn't," Shanon insisted. "I wanted to help Palmer. Where is she, anyway?"

"Outside," Amy said, "sitting on the back steps, staring at the sunset. You'd think she was at a funeral."

"Her own," Lisa added.

Shanon shook her head. "Let's go join her. Before we were interrupted, John told me something interesting about Sam. I think Palmer should know."

Palmer was right where Amy and Lisa had last seen her, slumped on the cement steps of Fox Hall. When she heard the girls come through the door, she turned aside.

"Go away!" she said. "I'm not in the mood for any gossip about your classes or how lovely the weather is and all that stuff."

Lisa sat down beside her. "Shanon has some news about Sam."

"How many times do I have to tell you? I don't want to hear anything about that creep!" Palmer fumed. "Just leave me alone."

Shanon took a deep breath. She'd gone to a lot of trouble to find out the truth. The least Palmer could do was listen to it. "Sam *was* a student at Ardsley last semester," Shanon began, "just as we'd suspected from the photo Rob sent. But he dropped out, and he goes to Brighton High now."

Palmer clapped her hands over her ears. "I can't hear you!"

"Shout," Lisa advised Shanon. "I'm sure she can still hear."

Shanon stepped closer to Palmer and raised her normally

90

soft voice. "He really is a rock singer. John says so. And he's going to be at the mixer tomorrow night."

"I don't care," Palmer declared, dropping her hands.

Lisa thought for a second. "Palmer, until you face Sam and talk this thing out, you won't be happy. And no matter what you say to us, you won't really be through with him!"

To her suitemates' surprise, Palmer didn't argue this point. "I think you're right," she exclaimed after a few minutes of silence.

Lisa blinked. "You do?"

"I do," Palmer repeated, getting to her feet in one swift motion. "I've changed my mind. I'm going to that dance— and I'm going to tell Mr. Sam O'Leary just what I think of him." And with a satisfied smile, Palmer turned on her heel and went back into Fox Hall, leaving her three friends staring at each other.

Lisa chewed her bottom lip. "I hope we haven't just made a bad situation worse."

"Me too," Amy agreed, turning to Shanon. But Shanon didn't say a word. She was too busy worrying about her own bad situation. If only she had refused to go near the *Ledger* computer. . . .

CHAPTER ELEVEN

All four Foxes were up bright and early Saturday morning, the day of the Ardsley mixer. Amy and Lisa were much too happy to sleep, Shanon was too nervous, and Palmer was . . . well, Palmer was just Palmer!

By the time the afternoon rolled around and they were getting ready for the dance, Suite 3-D was charged with excitement. Palmer flew around the room she shared with Amy, tossing a steady stream of shoes and dresses out of her closet, rejecting them all.

Shanon, who'd decided that whatever punishment Miss Pryn had in store for her probably wouldn't be handed out until after the weekend, peeked through the doorway. "You'd look nice in any of them," she told Palmer encouragingly.

"Tonight," Palmer proclaimed, "nice is not enough. I want to look absolutely gorgeous—so Sam can see exactly what he's missing."

"Oh, my," Shanon sighed, closing Palmer's door behind her.

Lisa and Amy were waiting in the sitting room. Lisa had chosen a short black tube skirt with a long sequined T-shirt and clunky black shoes. Amy wore a black satin jumpsuit with a wide, shocking pink cummerbund and a matching bow in her moussed hair.

"How's Palmer doing?" Lisa asked, keeping her voice low.

Shanon shook her head. "She still hasn't picked an outfit."

Just then, there was a firm knock on the hallway door. Lisa got up to answer it.

"Hi, everyone." Kate Majors stepped into the sitting room. She was wearing a bright red dress that brought a becoming glow to her usually pale complexion. Her face flushed even more as she handed Shanon a square white envelope addressed to Palmer. "This was delivered to the *Ledger* office for some reason," she explained. "I thought maybe I'd better deliver it by hand, seeing as how . . ." She shrugged.

It seemed that the story of Palmer's latest misadventure had leaked out. All of Fox Hall was abuzz with rumors about Palmer and her rock star.

Kate handed the envelope to Shanon, who stared at it, then at Palmer's closed door. "It's from Sam," she said to Lisa, her eyes widening. "Oh, here. *You* take it. I can't give it to her!"

Lisa took the envelope and studied the clean, neat script.

93

Sam's return address was on the upper left corner, only this time it was a street in Brighton, not a dorm at Ardsley.

With a determined step, Lisa crossed the room to Palmer's door and rapped lightly.

"Go away! I'm getting dressed."

"There's a letter here for you," Lisa called through the door. "It's from Sam."

The door swung open. Palmer had chosen a dazzling pale blue dress that just skimmed her knees. She picked an invisible piece of lint off the skirt before snatching the envelope out of Lisa's hand.

"You might as well see what he has to say," Kate advised. "Things can't get any worse than they already are."

"You're probably right," Palmer said as she tore open the flap.

Dear Palmer,

I'm writing because a friend of mine has been bugging me, saying I owe you an explanation. So, here goes. . . . Last winter, after I transferred from Ardsley Academy to the high school in town, I kept getting the Ardsley newspaper. I saw your ad for a pen pal. You probably don't remember me, but I sure remembered you. I saw you at the Halloween dance and wanted to meet you then, but you were with some other guy.

Anyway, I figured from your ad he was no longer in the picture, and now was my chance. But the advertisement said you wanted an Ardie to write to you. Well, since I really had *been at Ardsley, I decided I'd just pretend I was still there.*

A friend from my old dorm helped me out—Arthur Martinez. He was the only one of your roommates' pen pals who knew me. Mars arranged to pick up my mail from the Ardsley mail room and then passed it on to me. (Don't blame him for not telling you the whole truth about me—I made him promise to keep my secret. But that was only because I was afraid you wouldn't write to me. Mars also told me how much money your family in Palm Beach has.)

Anyway, everything I wrote to you was true. I do sing rock and roll. I like sports, but I play on the public school teams now. I also work weekends at the Shoe Emporium in the mall because my *family doesn't have much money at all, and the little bit my band gets for playing gigs around here is barely enough to keep us in guitar picks and sheet music.*

I was afraid that once you found out I wasn't some rich preppie, you'd dump me fast. That day you saw me at the mall, you sure took off like a rocket. Guess I wasn't exactly what you were looking for.

At first I was upset because things didn't work out between us, Palmer. But now that I know what a snob you are, I'm glad we never really had a date.

Signed,
Sam

Palmer crumpled the note into a ball and threw it across

95

the room. "I don't believe it!" she squeaked. "A snob! Imagine him calling *me* a snob!"

Lisa and Amy exchanged glances. There was a time when they would have given Sam a round of applause for putting their suitemate in her place. Palmer was the queen of snobs—at least she had been when she first moved into Suite 3-D in September. Now, however, Lisa wasn't so sure.

"Just think," Palmer muttered, "I gave up my two free afternoons each week, all semester long, to tutor some little kid from Brighton, probably his next-door neighbor. And he calls me a *snob!*"

"Maybe if he got to know you a little better," Lisa suggested.

"Hah!" Palmer snorted. "That'll be the day. All he's going to get to know of me is my opinion of him! And that's not much. Come on, Foxes. Let's go dancing!"

CHAPTER TWELVE

The Ardsley Academy gymnasium had been transformed into a wonderland. A rainbow arch of balloons rose above the bandstand, where several musicians were tuning up their instruments. Girls in springtime pastel dresses or hot bright colors ready for summer gossiped in groups and watched the boys who'd gathered around the long, crepe paper–decorated refreshment table.

The huge speakers on either side of the bandstand crackled as the girls from Fox Hall walked into the gym. A guitar whined wildly.

"Ooh," Amy said, her eyes alert, searching the stage for whoever had produced the high-pitched feedback. "I bet he's good."

"I wonder where our dates are," Lisa said.

Shanon's cheeks flushed at the thought of Mars. "I don't see them anywhere. Maybe they're not here yet. We're a little early."

"I don't see how you can even speak to Mars," Palmer

complained bitterly. "He knew all about Sam and didn't even tell me."

Lisa squeezed Palmer's hand. "He was just keeping a promise to a friend. I don't think he realized you'd get hurt. When it started out, all Sam wanted was to write to you."

"Forget about Sam, Palmer," Amy suggested. "Now that we're here, how about cooling it? Try to enjoy yourself."

"No way." Palmer shook her blond mane. "I'm going to give Sam a piece of my mind for what he did to me."

"Hey, look!" Amy cried. "The guitarists all play Fenders. Those are the greatest guitars on earth. Oh, come on, let's get closer to the stage. I want to see them."

Grabbing Shanon by the hand, Amy took off across the polished wood floor.

"We might as well go with them," Lisa pointed out. "You can stalk your prey from the other side of the room as well as from here."

Palmer shrugged. "Why not?"

Amy ogled the shiny red-and-black electric guitars that were now resting on metal stands on the stage. "The band will be back any minute for their first set," she informed the others. "I heard someone say they were just about to start."

"Hi, Foxes!"

The girls spun around as Rob, Mars, and John cut through another group of Alma students and came up behind them.

98

"Hi, Rob," Lisa said. "This is really great. I mean, the decorations and all."

"Glad you like them. Mars and I spent the afternoon filling the balloons with helium."

"It's a beautiful rainbow," Shanon said, stepping closer to Mars.

He smiled at her, but when he caught sight of Palmer, he dropped his glance.

"Traitor," Palmer muttered, just loud enough for Mars to hear.

"Palmer, I . . . I'm sorry," Mars said, turning bright red. "I didn't think there was anything wrong with helping Sam meet you."

John stepped forward. "He was just trying to help out a friend."

"Some friend!" Palmer exclaimed, giving Mars a withering look.

"Now, calm down, Palmer," Lisa soothed. "Save it for Sam. He's supposed to be here tonight."

"If he dares show his face," Palmer said in disgust.

Lisa turned to Rob. "That part's true, isn't it? He *will* be here?"

Rob exchanged a hasty glance with Mars and John. "Yeah. Any minute."

Just then, the lights in the gym flickered and went out. A couple of girls squealed.

"It's the band, making their entrance," Amy whispered excitedly in the dark, as footsteps pounded across the platform.

A moment later, a spotlight hit the stage and a wild drum roll thundered through the gym. Three guitarists, a keyboard player, one saxophone player, and the drummer ripped into a loud rock number.

"Oh," Amy sighed, "they're *really* good." She looked up at John. "I could listen to them all night."

Mars reached bashfully for Shanon's hand. "Want to dance?"

She gave him a shy smile. "Absolutely."

Rob stepped over close to Lisa, and she swallowed nervously. He was the nicest, greatest-looking boy she'd ever known.

"Well?" he asked, his blue eyes sparkling in the shadowy gym.

Lisa giggled and put her hand in his. "Sure, I'd love to dance," she murmured. But on second thought, she turned to Palmer, not sure it was right to leave her alone.

Palmer looked as if she'd turned to stone. She stood frozen in one spot, her face rigid, eyes wide with shock.

"Palmer, what's wrong?"

Her suitemate didn't answer. Then Lisa followed Palmer's gaze up onto the stage, past the guitarists to the boy on the drums. She knew that face. She'd seen it in a photograph—and in Suzy's Shoe Emporium!

"Oh, my gosh!" Lisa gasped. "It's Sam O'Leary."

Palmer was still staring silently up at the stage. She didn't seem aware of anyone but Sam.

Rob tugged on Lisa's hand. "She really is upset, isn't she?"

"You could say that," Lisa answered. "If I were Sam, I think I'd stay up on that stage all night."

"Poor Sam!" Rob chuckled. But Palmer was the one he really felt sorry for. Her face was unnaturally pink—whether from anger or embarrassment, he couldn't tell for sure.

Lisa felt torn. She wanted to do something to make Palmer feel better—and she really wanted to dance with Rob. After the opening number, the band would probably do something slow. She'd give anything to be out on the dance floor, ready to move into Rob's arms on the first soft chord. But then there was Palmer. . . .

"We'd better stay close," she said, nodding at her friend.

Rob led her only a few steps away before starting to dance.

At the end of the first number, the band members gathered in the middle of the stage for a quick huddle. One of the guitarists put down his instrument and took Sam's place at the drums.

Palmer had been watching every move Sam made through narrowed eyes. From the moment she'd first seen him in the spotlight, her knees had felt weak. Then, as she'd watched him perform, something inside her had seemed to give way. She stared at Sam, unable to take her eyes off him.

"He's the most gorgeous boy I've ever seen," she murmured, unaware that Lisa and the others had moved out of hearing range.

Sam's pale, reddish-blond hair looked fantastic in the

101

spotlight. He really was great looking, and talented, and . . . just about perfect! If only he hadn't been so dishonest with her from the start. He'd really hurt her, and she didn't know if she could ever forgive him.

At the end of the first number, Palmer turned and started to walk sadly away from the stage.

The band struck up the slow, romantic strains of one of Lisa's favorite songs. For a moment, Rob looked unsure of himself.

Lisa giggled. "We don't have to, if you don't want to," she said.

"No," he answered quickly, "it's not that. I just thought maybe you'd want to dance with some of the other boys . . . some of the time. I didn't want you to think I'd be upset, if you did."

"Well, if you put it that way . . ." She pretended to ponder her options, glancing around at the Ardsley boys grouped on one side of the room. But when Rob began to look uncomfortable, she gave him a wide grin. "Just teasing. I want to dance with *you*."

He smiled happily. "That's great, Lisa. I didn't want to dance with anyone else either."

His arms had just come around her when she saw Palmer heading for the gymnasium door.

Lisa looked up at Rob with a troubled frown. "I have to go to Palmer. She needs me."

"She'll be all right. See, Sam is going after her. Let them work it out."

As Lisa turned, she saw Sam leap lightly down from the

stage and take off at a run after Palmer. "I don't know . . ." Lisa said, chewing her bottom lip nervously.

Palmer was already in the middle of the floor, pushing blindly through the dancers, when Sam caught up with her.

"Hey, Palmer, wait up!"

"Leave me alone," she cried, tears streaming down her cheeks.

He grabbed her arm and spun her around, then stepped back as if he didn't know what to do next. He shuffled from foot to foot while she waited for him to go on.

"I—I don't get it," he finally said, stammering under her teary blue gaze. "What's the big deal? *You* dumped *me*. Remember? Why are you so upset?"

"That's not how it happened at all," Palmer sniffed. "When you turned down my invitation to the geology seminar, I thought you'd dumped me. Then I saw you at the shoe store and found out you weren't even an Ardsley student. I figured you were just playing a joke on me—to be mean."

Sam stared at her, his mouth open in shock. "I would never do a thing like that."

"Well, that's how it seemed," Palmer sputtered. "Then you wrote that letter and called me a snob. I'm not a snob. I have three friends who'll tell you that. And there's a little girl in Brighton that I tutor twice a week—on my own time. Maybe I sometimes get hung up on clothes and cars and stuff like that. But that doesn't give you the right to insult me! I never did anything to you."

Sam took a deep breath, for courage. He seemed unsure

103

of what to say or do. Then soft music swelled from the bandstand, and all around them boys and girls swayed to the romantic sound.

"I'm sorry, Palmer," he said. "I didn't mean to hurt your feelings. But you hurt mine. When you ran away from the shoe store, I figured you just didn't want anything to do with a boy from town who had to work and couldn't afford to go to Ardsley anymore. Mars said you were bragging all over the Alma campus that I was a rich rock star. I knew I could never live up to that, if that was what you wanted."

She bit her lip and looked at Sam.

"I still want to be your pen pal," he said.

"I don't know," she murmured. "The things you said . . . they were really mean. I don't think I can just forget them."

"Please, Palmer," Sam said, his gray eyes pleading.

She shook her head mutely and started to walk away. Lisa, Amy, and Shanon had been watching Palmer and Sam from a distance. Now they edged across the room and formed a protective circle around her.

"We told the boys that we'd go back to Alma with you, if that's what you want," Lisa said.

Palmer looked at each of them, her eyes shining with tears. "Thanks," she said. "You're all such good friends."

The song came to an end. As the crowd clapped, Sam looked dismally up at his band, his heart no longer in this gig. Then he thought of something—something that just might convince Palmer he wasn't such a bad guy after all.

Running through the crowd, he jumped up onto the

104

stage and quickly consulted the other band members. Then he picked up his electric guitar and stepped to the microphone.

"The next song," he announced nervously, "is dedicated to the most beautiful girl I know. She'd also make a great friend, if she'd just forgive me for being really dumb. I don't want to embarrass her by saying her name, but I'm sure she knows who she is. . . ."

Halfway out the gymnasium door, Palmer turned and stared at Sam on the stage. He was looking straight at her, his gray eyes begging her to come back.

"Oh!" Shanon gasped. "How romantic!"

Lisa touched Palmer encouragingly on the arm. "It sounds like he really means it."

Confused, Palmer looked at her roommate Amy. "What should I do?"

Amy laughed. "Go for it!"

Slowly, Palmer made her way back across the dance floor, between smiling couples, as Sam sang a love song— just for her.

CHAPTER THIRTEEN

Dear Rob,

Thanks for a wonderful mixer. I especially liked the decorations. They were beautiful. Of course, I also liked dancing with you. I just wish we were allowed to have later, longer dances—like until midnight or one o'clock. Did you ever see that old musical, My Fair Lady? *It's kind of sappy, but I like it anyway. There's a song in it, "I Could Have Danced All Night." That's just about how I felt when we got back to Fox Hall.*

Still dancing,
Lisa

Dear John,

Last night was super! I got to see you, plus I met Sam and his group. Wasn't it neat how he offered to try out one of our songs next time The Fantasy has a gig? I've been thinking about that. Let's write one specially for them! We can call it "Fantasy," and give it a really wild drum riff to match their style. What do you say?

Signed,
I-feel-the-beat Amy!

Dear Mars,

I know you feel a little guilty for what happened between Sam and Palmer, but it wasn't your fault. Being loyal to a friend is important, and you had no way of knowing things would get so weird.

I can't believe what a great time I had at the mixer. I thought I'd be too worried about my computer "crime" to enjoy it, but being with you is so much fun I almost forgot about the whole awful mess. Almost! Now that I'm back at Alma again, I can't stop wondering what's going to happen. Whatever it is, I wish Miss Pryn would let me know soon.

Did I tell you how much I love the giant paper clip you gave me? Who would ever guess you could make something like that out of an old coat hanger! Anyway, I think it's really clever. Only trouble is, it's so heavy, it sort of bends regular paper. So I'm using it for a wall decoration, over my bed near your picture. Lisa says it looks like some kind of modern sculpture. Palmer says maybe you'll become a famous artist one day. Her mother has a sculpture in her garden made up entirely of old car parts; she says it cost thousands of dollars. Do you believe that?

Sincerely,
Shanon

Dear Palmer,

I just got home from the Big Mix. It took us over an hour to load the instruments and sound system into my dad's truck, then drop the guys off at their homes. It's almost two a.m., but I still can't get to sleep. I keep thinking about you.

I'm so glad we worked everything out. I should have known a great girl like you couldn't be so shallow she'd dump a boy just because he wasn't rich. What a humongous idiot I am, huh? Anyway, I had to write you this very minute to tell you how happy I am to be your pen pal, again.

Yours for keeps,
Sam

Dear Sam,

I have a confession to make. You weren't all that far wrong about me—I mean what you said about dumping a boy because of money. I do have kind of a hang-up about expensive clothes and cars and stuff like that. Guess I never really thought much about it until I came to Alma Stephens. But living with my roommates, and then meeting you, is beginning to change the way I think about a lot of things.

Anyway, you don't need money—I have enough for both of us. Ha, ha!

Seriously though, you said at the dance that you'd like to hear more about the little girl I'm tutoring—Gabby. Well, it turns out she's really smart, not at all slow like I thought. It's just that she gets distracted real easy (sort of the way I

108

am with homework), so I have to think of super-inventive ways to keep her attention.

Hey! I've got a fantastic idea! Why don't you drop by the library after you get out of school some Tuesday or Thursday. That is, if you're not working. I meet with Gabby from two to three. Sometimes Miss Grayson gives us fifteen minutes to check out a book after we're done tutoring. Maybe we could look for one, together. Anyway, I'd really like to see you again—very soon!

Most, most sincerely,
Palmer

"You *have* been doing a fantastic job with Gabby," Shanon said when Palmer finished reading the letter she'd written to Sam. "You should be very proud of yourself."

"I am," Palmer admitted, slipping the sheet of paper into its envelope. "This is the first time I've ever really done anything to help someone."

"Come on," Lisa said. "That's not true."

"Oh, yeah," Palmer challenged. "Name one time I did something for you guys without your begging me."

Lisa, Shanon, and Amy all started to protest at once. And all at once, the three fell silent.

Palmer laughed. "See?"

Shanon shook her head. "You're not a selfish person, Palmer. Not deep down. You just didn't know how to be . . ." She frowned, fishing for a tactful word.

"Nice? Considerate? Neat?" Amy supplied, perhaps thinking of all the times she'd had to pick up after her roommate.

Palmer sighed. "In my old school, everyone was just like me. All the kids ever talked about was going shopping or who was having the next party or how big a yacht their dad had. I didn't know that friends—real friends, like you three—could be so great." She lowered her head bashfully, her blond hair spilling forward over her eyes. "And now I have Sam, too. I can't believe how well everything's worked out."

Lisa smiled from her end of the pink loveseat and put an arm around Palmer's shoulders. "I think you've finally qualified as one of the gang."

The other two girls nodded in agreement.

"Definitely," Shanon murmured.

There was a knock on the door.

"I'll get it!" Amy shouted, bouncing to her feet.

She swung the door wide. Dolores Countee stood in the hallway, and suddenly Suite 3-D fell silent.

"I'm here to see Shanon," Dolores announced.

With a worried glance at her friends, Shanon stood up and crossed the room. "Y-yes?" she stammered.

The tall redhead gave Shanon a stern look. "Miss Pryn just called. She wants to see us in her office right away."

Shanon swallowed. She had no doubt about the reason for the summons. Shakily, she stood up and started toward the door.

"Do you want us to go with you?" Lisa asked.

"After all, it was partly our fault," Amy said. "We asked you to do it."

"And you were only trying to help me," Palmer added.

"No," said Shanon, her hazel eyes dull. "I could have refused."

"That's right," Dolores said sharply. "You knew the rules, and you broke them anyway. The Foxes can't get you out of this one, Shanon Davis."

Shanon nodded sadly. It was true. Nothing anyone could do now would help. She only hoped Miss Pryn hadn't telephoned her parents, or, worse yet, that the steely-haired headmistress wouldn't take away her scholarship—or suspend her from school altogether! She hadn't mentioned these fears to her suitemates. She hadn't wanted to take away from their excitement over the mixer. But ever since Dolores had caught her at the computer, Shanon had been worrying and wondering what would happen to her. Now, as she followed Dolores out of the room and down the stairs of her beloved Fox Hall, she couldn't help thinking that her days there might soon be over.

As the door closed behind their suitemate, Lisa, Amy, and Palmer stood in the middle of the sitting room, staring at each other in dismay.

"I can't believe it," said Lisa.

"What with trying to straighten out all this Sam business, we completely forgot about poor Shanon."

"I feel so terrible," Palmer moaned. "What do you think will happen to her?"

"I don't even want to think about it."

Amy kicked a black sandal at the air in disgust. "She might get thrown out of school, but it isn't fair. She shouldn't get in trouble. She was just trying to help a friend."

Lisa's lower lip quivered. "The Foxes of the Third Dimension wouldn't be the same without her," she whispered.

Amy looked as if she were going to cry.

"Well," Palmer said, squaring her shoulders. "I, for one, am not going to stand by while Shanon gets booted out of Alma."

"What are you going to do?" Amy asked.

"Call my father," Palmer said firmly, starting for the door.

Lisa stepped in front of her. "What can he do?"

"Plenty." Palmer's blue eyes were bright. "He's a big contributor to the Alma Stephens scholarship fund. All he has to do is threaten Miss Pryn with taking his money away if she makes Shanon leave, and . . ." She shrugged. "Well, she'll just have to let her stay."

"Don't you think that's a little drastic?" Lisa asked.

"Not to mention illegal!" Amy added. "Or haven't you heard that blackmail's a federal offense?"

Palmer faced her friends with her hands on her hips. "Well, what do *you* suggest we do?"

It took a full ten minutes for Dolores and Shanon to walk across the sunny campus to the administration building. As soon as they entered the headmistress's outer office, the secretary waved them through.

Miss Pryn looked up with a grim expression. "Sit down, girls. I'll be right with you."

Shanon felt sick to her stomach. In the fall, the campus had seemed so different from her old school. Because she was shy, she'd worried about making friends. She'd worried about a lot of things. But living with Lisa, Amy, and Palmer had made her braver in many ways—maybe too brave this time. Oh, she really didn't want to leave Alma Stephens.

Shanon looked down at her hands. At last, she couldn't stand the silence, and she peeked up from under her long brown lashes. Miss Pryn was staring straight at her, wide suited shoulders stiff, mouth drawn into a firm line.

"Do you know why you're here, Shanon?" the headmistress asked.

"Yes, ma'am," Shanon murmured, her throat painfully tight.

"Dolores was very upset when she came to me on Friday."

"I suppose she was," Shanon said miserably.

"She's responsible for running *The Ledger* on a tight budget. Computer time is expensive."

"But I only used it a couple of times," Shanon explained, "for just a few minutes. And they were emergencies."

"Emergencies?"

Dolores broke in. "She's lying. I caught her chatting with her Ardsley pen pal."

Shanon gasped, tears stinging her eyes. "No. Honest, Miss Pryn, it was really important. I only—"

Just then, there was a commotion in the outer office. Shanon could hear the receptionist's raised voice. "No, you absolutely cannot go in there. You'll have to wait," she cried as Miss Pryn's door flew open and Lisa, Amy, and Palmer tumbled in.

For a moment, no one said anything. Miss Pryn sat solemnly behind her desk, staring at the three intruders. They stood like statues, staring back.

Lisa was the first to speak. "Miss Pryn," she began in a breathless voice, "we apologize for interrupting, but we all feel ..." She looked around at her roommates. "Well, we're as much to blame as Shanon for using the computer."

"Explain, please," Miss Pryn said.

Palmer stepped forward and went on to tell Miss Pryn all about her misunderstanding with Sam, and how upset she'd been. "So, you see," she finished, "Shanon was just trying to get one of the boys at Ardsley to help, to try to straighten everything out—for me."

Dolores shot to her feet. "That doesn't excuse her for breaking the rules! Someone has been spending a whole lot of unauthorized time on the computer. And I caught *her*, red-handed!"

"Shanon?" Miss Pryn asked.

"It wasn't me the other times. I swear," Shanon said sincerely. "I love working at *The Ledger*. I wouldn't do anything to hurt the newspaper."

Dolores sighed, shaking her head. "I have to admit, Shanon's one of my most cooperative and responsible staff members."

"Do you have any proof that she was using the computer during the other times you were billed?" Miss Pryn asked.

"No," Dolores admitted reluctantly. "I just assumed

since I caught her this time that she was . . . you know . . . the one."

Shanon drew a deep breath, feeling a little braver now. "Am I going to be able to stay on at Alma? Can I keep my scholarship?"

Miss Pryn leaned back in her chair and observed Shanon for a long, silent minute. "Of course," she finally said. "You're a good student, Shanon. You've become a valuable part of the school."

Shanon beamed.

"But, despite your admirable loyalty to your friend," the headmistress went on, "Dolores is right—you have broken a serious rule. And so, for the remainder of the month, you'll be off *The Ledger* staff. After that, you may resume your usual duties. From now on, however, you'll need to clear all computer time directly with Dolores. Every minute. Do you understand?"

Shanon nodded happily.

Dolores stepped forward. "I'm sorry I suspected you, Shanon," she murmured. "I just assumed . . ."

"That's okay." Shanon smiled. "I guess it looked pretty bad. Besides, I should have asked you first." Shanon turned shyly to Miss Pryn. "May we go now?"

"Certainly," the headmistress said kindly.

As soon as they were outside, the four Foxes squealed and hugged each other. It was several minutes before any of them realized that Dolores was still there. They turned to her, not sure what to expect.

"Listen, I've got an idea," Dolores said in a thoughtful

115

voice. "I really want to make this up to you, Shanon. I know how much the Brighton Project means to you, so I was thinking—maybe *The Ledger* could do a feature story on the tutoring program. You know, with pictures and little interviews of a few of the third-graders and their tutors."

"Oh, that would be wonderful!" Shanon cried.

"Photos?" Palmer asked, her eyes sparkling. "You've got to warn us when the pictures will be taken. I mean, I'll have to think about what to wear." She rested her chin on one hand and considered. "If I had a little extra time, I could do Gabby's hair—straighten it out or something. Maybe we could even wear matching outfits. . . . What do you think?"

"Oh, no!" Dolores teased as she turned to leave them. "Watch out. A new junior, junior deb in the making!"

"This is too much!" Lisa squealed. "Shanon gets to stay. The Brighton Project gets a photo spread! We've *got* to celebrate!"

Amy giggled. "How about we split the cost on a super-large, everything-on-it Monstro pizza from Figaro's!"

"You're on!" cried Shanon.

"While we wait for the za-wagon to come," Palmer suggested, referring to their favorite pizza place's delivery van, "we can start the party with some dancing."

Lisa laughed. "I bet you're going to suggest a special tape—something by a new group called The Fantasy?"

Palmer grinned. "How'd you guess?"

A few minutes later, Palmer's stereo had been moved out

into the sitting room of Suite 3-D, plugged in, and the coffee table shoved out of the way. The four girls bounced to the beat of Sam O'Leary's band.

"You know," Lisa shouted over the guitars, "I've decided that going to an all-girls school isn't so bad, not with friends like you guys."

"Let's be suitemates next year too!" Amy yelled over the crashing drums.

The four girls smiled at each other, knowing that they were all thinking the same thing at that moment. All together, they shouted it out: "Foxes of the Third Dimension—forever!"

Something to write home about . . .
                              three new Pen Pals stories!

*In Book Six, Amy, Palmer, Lisa, and Shanon go on a class
trip to London. Amy is especially excited because she has
plans to meet with an English musician who wants to hear
her sing! It will be her English debut. The trouble is, she
can't get permission to go. The musician plays in a little
restaurant called the Sandwich Board, not far from the
theater where the girls will be seeing Shakespeare's* Hamlet.
Here is a scene from Pen Pals #6: AMY'S SONG

Some time later the rest of the Alma group boarded the
bus, and before long they arrived at the park in front of the
Royal Shakespeare Theatre. The view of the River Avon
was lovely. Lisa, Shanon, Palmer, and Amy sat on a bench
near the water, each with a box lunch balanced on her lap.

"At least it hasn't rained," Shanon said, trying to sound cheerful.

"Right," Amy said expressionlessly.

"It just isn't fair!" Palmer fumed. "Something important like a debut and you have to miss it!"

"Miss Grayson did say there was a slim chance of going to the Sandwich Board for tea," Shanon volunteered.

"Fat chance," said Amy. "Ever since I asked to go, they've kept telling me maybe. I'm sure it won't be any different after we get out of the theater."

Lisa took out her map of Stratford-upon-Avon again. "What street did you say the restaurant is on?" she asked.

"High Street," said Amy.

"That's so silly," exclaimed Lisa. "It's probably only five minutes from here!"

"So what?" Amy sighed. "We still can't go."

"I'm not so sure about that," Lisa muttered. She looked at Shanon. "Did you ever read *Hamlet*?"

"Sure," said Shanon. "I read the whole thing."

"Is it a long play?" asked Lisa.

Shanon nodded. "Very. It's also one of my favorites. There's a ghost in it."

Lisa's eyes gleamed mischievously. Just behind them was the theater. "I bet there are lots of scenes in it," she said. "Lots of chances for stepping out of the theater."

Amy's mouth dropped open. "Are you thinking what I think you're thinking?"

"I think so," Lisa said.

Shanon gasped. "You wouldn't!"

Palmer giggled. "Sounds like fun."

"I don't know," Amy said doubtfully.

Lisa shrugged. "Why not? It's just like sneaking into the kitchen at night back at Alma."

"I think it's a little more serious than that," said Shanon shakily.

"So is Amy's English debut," Lisa argued. She turned to Amy. "So . . . what do you say?"

Amy looked at the map. What harm could it do to sneak out of *Hamlet*? High Street was just minutes away. No one would even know they were gone. Unless of course, they got caught. . . .

Can Amy pull it off? Or will she have to miss her big break? Find out in Pen Pals #6!

PEN PALS #7:   HANDLE WITH CARE

Shanon is tired of standing in Lisa's shadow. She wants to be thought of as her own person. So she decides to run for student council representative—against Lisa! Lisa not only feels abandoned by her best friend, but by her pen pal, too. While the election seems to be bringing Shanon and Mars closer together, it's definitely driving Lisa and Rob apart. Lisa's sure she'll win the election. After all, she's always been a leader—shy Shanon's the follower. Or is she? Will the election spoil the girls' friendship? And will it mean the end of Rob and Lisa?

PEN PALS #8:   SEALED WITH A KISS

When the Ardsley and Alma drama departments join forces to produce a rock musical, Lisa and Amy audition just for fun. Lisa lands a place in the chorus, but Amy gets a leading role. Lisa can't help feeling a little jealous, especially when her pen pal Rob also gets a leading role—opposite Amy. To make matters worse, the director wants Rob and Amy to kiss! Amy is so caught up in the play that she doesn't notice Lisa's jealousy—at first. And when she finally does notice, the damage has already been done!

P.S. Have you missed any _Pen Pals_? Catch up now!

PEN PALS #1: BOYS WANTED!

Suitemates Lisa, Shanon, Amy, and Palmer love the Alma Stephens School for Girls. There's only one problem—no boys! So the girls put an ad in the newspaper of the nearby Ardsley Academy for Boys asking for male pen pals. Soon their mailboxes are flooded with letters and photos from Ardsley boys, but the girls choose four boys from a suite just like their own. Through their letters, the girls learn a lot about their new pen pals—and about themselves.

PEN PALS #2: TOO CUTE FOR WORDS

Palmer, the rich girl from Florida, has never been one for playing by the rules. So when she wants Amy's pen pal, Simmie, instead of her own, she simply takes him. She writes to Simmie secretly, and soon he stops writing to Amy. When Shanon, Lisa, and Amy find out why, the suite is in an uproar. How could Palmer be so deceitful? Before long, Palmer is thinking of leaving the suite—and the other girls aren't about to stop her. Where will it all end?

PEN PALS #3: P.S. FORGET IT!

Palmer is out to prove that her pen pal is the best—and her suitemate Lisa's is a jerk. When Lisa receives strange letters and a mysterious prank gift, it looks as if Palmer may be right. But does she have to be so smug about it? Soon it's all-out war in Suite 3-D.

From the sidelines, Shanon and Amy think something fishy is going on. Is the pen pal scheme going too far? Will it stop before Lisa does something she may regret? Or will the girls learn to settle their differences?

PEN PALS #4: NO CREEPS NEED APPLY

Palmer takes up tennis so she can play in the Alma-Ardsley tennis tournament with her pen pal, Simmie Randolph III. Lisa helps coach Palmer, and soon Palmer has come so far that they are both proud of her. But when Palmer finds herself playing *against*—not *with*—her super-competitive pen pal, she realizes that winning the game could mean losing *him*!

Palmer wants to play her best, and her suitemates will think she's a real creep if she lets down the school. Is any boy worth the loss of her friends?